I0684911

Xin Publishing

Different Minds Different Lives

A collection of short stories and fragments by

Grace Semmens
Marko Kavka
Callum Brazzo
Lovie Lovetree
Jack Stocker
Tracey Hatlen Sakalis
Stephen Oldroyd
Rosie Jones
Harry Wells
John Gathercole
Merrill Stenton
Meryem B
Aidan Semmens
&
Clive Semmens

Edited by M H He

Xin Publishing

Published by Xin Publishing
an imprint of Xin He Ltd.
The Wonder Inn
29 Shudehill
Manchester
M4 2AF
United Kingdom

http://www.xin-publishing.uk/

Text ©   Grace Semmens, Marko Kavka,
            Callum Brazzo, Lovie Lovetree,
            Jack Stocker, Tracey Hatlen Sakalis,
            Stephen Oldroyd, Rosie Jones, Harry Wells,
            John Gathercole, Merrill Stenton,
            Meryem B, Aidan Semmens
            & Clive Semmens 2016
Cover ©   Fern Goodliffe, Wayland Goodliffe
            & Clive Semmens 2016

ISBN: 978-3-942357-26-5

Contents

Suchita

Grace

Once upon a time, a woman called Suchita lived in a little village. She had a baby daughter called Sanjita, whom she loved very much. She had to work very hard to get enough money for food; she was very poor. Her house was made of wood, plastered with a mixture of mud and dung. The roof hadn't any tiles, only straw. In summer it was very hot. She had no shoes, and when the ground got very hot she could feel the sand hot under her feet, and would sometimes get blisters.

One day Suchita went to collect bidi leaves to sell. She left Sanjita at home. As she was coming home, she saw that her house was on fire. She ran to the house as fast as she could because Sanjita was inside. She never thought about herself, she just ran in to save her baby. She bent over Sanjita to protect her, and ran outside.

Sanjita was unhurt, but Suchita was very badly burned. Her burns healed, but she was scarred all over, and her face became very ugly.

When Sanjita grew older, Suchita scraped together enough money to send her to a good boarding school. She visited her every Saturday.

Sanjita was very pretty, and she had lots of friends. When her friends saw how ugly her mother was, they teased her.

Sanjita was very sad, and decided not to see her mother any more. When Suchita came to see her, Sanjita sent a message with a friend, saying that she didn't want to see her. Suchita tried a few times to see Sanjita. She came and sat by the side of the road, close to the school hostel, and waited, and hoped her daughter would come by.

Eventually Suchita gave up hope, and stopped coming to try to see her daughter.

Nobody can begin to comprehend the sadness of that woman.

I am Still Here

Marko

I am old. I have been here from the Dawn of Mankind. I have seen mountains rising, lakes and rivers disappearing, forests turning old and dark.

I am thousands and thousands of years old. I do not remember how I got to be, only that at one moment, aeons ago, I simply was. For many years, I have just been watching, observing the world changing around me, not aware of what it is I was brought here to do. And, after all this time, I still don't know. But I have lived all along, being a part of this world; being a part of this world's changes. I walked the entire planet hundreds of times; feeling its pulse under my feet; inhaling its breath. I have set foot in the hidden parts of the globe, places unvisited by people even in their modern days.

I climbed every hilltop and every mountain peak. I swam in every ocean and every sea; touched every shore, brushed every tree. I was there, every time a volcano erupted; seen every storm and danced with every tornado.

And I am still here.

I remember clearly how excited I was when the humans started evolving, learning new tricks and passing their newly accumulated knowledge to their children. I lived among the animals of this planet for so long and yet, I could not foresee the potential of this specific species. From the shadows I have watched them create an easier, better life for themselves and their future generations. I enjoyed their success, I cried at their wars. For someone not human, I felt to be as much a part of them as I possibly could. They flourished. They travelled, expanding beyond their own limitations and expectations. The communities turned into tribes, then into villages, cities and states. They were many, and they divided themselves based on criteria I could not see or understand. Still, they progressed. For most of them, lives become easy and comfortable, though pointless. They drove around in machines, they flew higher than birds; they even left the gravitational embrace of this wonderful planet.

And then I watched them destroy it all in a blink.

It all happened so quickly. I have lived among them for a thousand years, and yet, I did not see it happening until it was too late. I watched them grow distant, from themselves and from the Nature they were a part of. For some reason, they wanted to escape their own roots, ignore the unity of mind and matter that works so flawlessly with everything else on this planet. They wanted more of everything by giving less and less. They dug their mines, extracting Earth's flesh; and laid their pipes, ever thirsty for her blood. And they never stopped, up till the very end.

They took everything and gave nothing in return.

I was there when the last generation of people that could enjoy the beauty of this planet forgot to teach their own children how to do it. It was but a blink of an eye for me, but I felt it and it hurt more than anything I have ever felt before. I was there when Nature took over, hurt and wounded as she was, trying to regain some control. People still fought her, even though many more would survive if they just realized what they have done.

I was there when balance shifted. I felt it in my core, for I was the part of this world as much it was the part of me. I could imagine Nature's tears as she did what she had to do. No matter what, the planet will survive. Human beings, slaves of their own comfort and technology, were nothing but collateral victims of a war they themselves created and had no chance of winning anyway.

I saw the fires, I felt the winds, and I endured the droughts and faced the ice at the end of it all, as I did many times before. Some of them survived, but most were simply wiped out. Eventually, in time… they were all gone.

I miss them, if that word applies to something as un-human as me. I thought they can do so much more good.

But I was wrong.

And I am still here.

Christmas and Autism

Callum

'It's nearly here!' screams Cally as she charges from her room upstairs to her Dad, Liam, who is sitting downstairs on the sofa with Tom.

At the sharp sound of Cally's tone, Tom curved his hands around his ears and buried his head in the comforting embrace of Dad.

'Careful talking, Cally, please' says Dad in a calm tone of voice.

'Oh, he's fine. At least he knows how to cover his ears. Could be worse, couldn't it really?' Cally responds.

'I am not sure 'worse' is the right word to use, Cally?' Dad gently questions.

'Well, it's like…you know…' said Cally as she drifted off and started to make herself a sandwich. Indeed, Dad did know. Dad knew that witnessing anything unfamiliar makes people curious and it was often tricky finding the words to explain Tom. Cally had spent enough Christmases with the family to form the opinion that Tom stood out like a sore thumb (that Tom would surely suck on if there actually WAS a thumb in front of him!)

At least Tom was getting attention, right? Was it the right attention?

Christmas was approaching in two days' time and Dad could see it now.

Family would gather, Tom included for as long as he could manage, then he would make a swift exit to the back garden to chew everything in sight.

Over the past years, many family members on his side of the family had openly spoken about Tom being a 'loner' compared with other children with some telling Dad to 'leave him to it.' Dad did not WANT to 'leave him to it' as his family, in Dad's mind, so negatively encouraged.

Dad had a feeling that, while it would be unadvised to force Tom to endure pain, there was still work to be done to ensure Tom got SOMETHING out of the festive season. And he was determined to find out how to make that happen.

With passion fuelling his rusty engine, Dad stroked Tom's hair softly and a smile shone on his face.

Lisa, Tom's Mother announced to the family, 'Mum is home!' Mum knew Tom needed routine and to anticipate change, therefore it would be beneficial to say her name as she entered a room so as not to cause any panic.

However, at Christmas, Mum struggled to cope with Tom. She felt a deep need to have Tom be part of the family gathering. Of course, there were additional social pressures placed on her by numerous members of her side of the family and she just wanted to understand why Tom hadn't grown out of it yet. 'What a glorious day that would be,' Mum thought to herself.

'Hello Cally. Hello Liam. Hello Tom,' said Mum.

All except Tom replied with their respective hellos.

Mum wore many scarves, this year's theme being red.

There were two purposes to this.

Firstly, Mum liked scarves. Secondly, they were worn to hide what had happened to Mum seemingly a decade ago, but in fact only two years ago.

Mum and Cally had an angry argument with Dad regarding Tom.

Mum and Cally believed that this Christmas was going to be the one where Tom would stop all his babyish behaviours like stuffing present wrapping in his mouth, ripping it to shreds and then spitting it out onto the previously clean floor. Mum and Cally were certain that Tom had gone for Mum's neck when yet more present wrapping was destroyed as a way of saying 'I will not be denied' but Dad had fought the corner of his son, albeit perhaps not strongly enough in Dad's mind. Dad defended Tom's actions by commanding Mum and Cally to 'Go easy on the boy, he's upset.'

'Yes and we know why he is upset. We're not letting him get what he wants' insisted Mum and Cally.

So when Mum came through the door, she took off her red scarf and all other outdoor clothes, put the kettle on, and then charged upstairs to immediately work on house maintenance. Matters concerning Christmas, like the gifts millions received on this day, were kept under wraps.

They could be left until tomorrow; Christmas Eve.

Each year, on Christmas Eve, the family took Tom to 'Lots Of Tots,' a local respite care home, for all its wonderful benefits. In addition to those identified factors, it served as an opportunity for all the other family members to execute their plan of action.

'Okay, so Tom's gone. Cally, have you got those sweets he likes?'

'Yes, I have the sweets.'

'Good, so he can enjoy them in the garden.'

'Wait a minute, could we maybe consider whether he could be WITH us this year?'

'Well, we've done that for at least two years now. We know he's probably if not definitely going to go outside so we can prepare, can't we Mum?'

'Absolutely! Good thinking, Cally.'

'Yes but what about the sugar intake?'

'Rubbish! He'll be fine with or without them.'

'It could affect him…'

'It does with most children.'

'That's true, Mum.'

'I read that it can be different with autistic…'

'Now STOP, please. He's a normal child who, when they don't get their own way, lashes out like he did last year with my neck, remember?'

'I don't want you hurt, I….'

Dad ceased pushing his side of the argument as a quick look at his phone told him it was time to collect Tom. Tom, as per usual, was happy to see Dad and they traveled home with ease. Dad and Tom went through their bedtime routine. An hour of play outside to allow time to readjust his sensory system (and to avoid any unfavourable behaviours brought on by the house's new look) before Tom was niftily led up to his bedroom, again, with Dad at his side. Mum and Cally were busy with decorating in the way the family had for years, even before Tom was born. After Tom had gone to sleep about 8PM, Dad thought to himself. He knew that millions of us in the world lived by routines but just this once; he wanted a change if not for his sake for Tom's. He laid next to Tom for the rest of the night. In that moment, Dad wanted to try something. He waited agonizingly for the day to end and his loving, yet perhaps misguided, family to come upstairs to sleep before he set to work on his plan.

*

It was Christmas Day, and Mum and Cally were tired but habitually awoke around seven, expecting Tom's screams and hollers of excitement. No sounds of this sort yet. That surprised Mum. 'Are you sure it's Christmas, Mum?'

'Is Dad with Tom?' Cally wondered.

'Of course' Mum replied.

''Well, I'll see you downstairs then, Mum.'

'Okay' said Mum as she snatched the overhanging scarf from the door.

Mum looked into Tom's room and, magically, Dad and Tom were not there.

Mum was stunned into momentary silence until reasoning shook her by the hand.

'Hmm. Must be downstairs already.'

Before she went downstairs to make Christmas drinks and to open presents, though Tom would likely favour the wrapping over whatever was inside, she heard 'Mum..' from Cally.

Mum entered, what she perceived to be, a bare room. No bright and cheery Elf decorations she had deliberately bought with Tom in her mind. Nothing of her design. Why?

She had her red scarf wrapped around her neck, perfectly fine but psychologically troubling, as she knelt to Tom's level on the floor. Tom was in between Dad's legs, playing with colourful piece of wrapping paper.

'I got him a spare piece, don't worry. He's happy playing with that.' Dad assures.

'What about the…the Elf...'

Tom suddenly spots the scarf and drops the wrapping paper. Moans begin.

'Oh, no. Just because I'm here, you silly boy. You're not..'

'Give him your scarf.'

'What? Mum can't do that Dad. Remember what he does?'

'Please, give Tom the scarf.

Something about this whole morning and Dad's concentrated gaze made Mum give in. She unwrapped her scarf, revealing today's gift.

Lisa very hesitantly outstretched her hand but before she could let go, Dad said firmly 'Say what it is then pass it to him, like this' said Dad as he demonstrated outstretching his hand and saying the word 'scarf.' Mum did as asked and Tom took its bright, cheery warmth into his body, slobbering all over it in pure glee. His happiness was unrestrained, thoroughly attached to the texture, the smell.

Mum, Cally and Dad watched this unfold.

'Ah, darn. He's slobbered all over it!' Cally exclaimed but Dad held a hand up, indicating that they should wait for this event to come to a natural close.

Tom finally looked up at his family, that had gathered together in awe and then, laughter and joy.

'Lisa.'

'Yes, Liam.'

'We need to talk about Tom and we need to change a few things.'

Sulwesi Adams

Clive

On the train to Delhi, we got into conversation with a young Indian man. It's a long journey, and we must have heard practically his whole life story.

His name was Sulwesi Adams. I should tell you how to say that: Sull (like pull) – way – ssy (like fussy).

If you think it's a funny name, you're not alone – it's a funny name to an Indian ear, too. His mother died when he was born, and his father left him and his big sister with the local missionary's wife, Mrs Adams. His father left the village, and they've never seen or heard of him since.

Sulwesi's sister has got a sensible name, Prema, because she had it already. But Mrs Adams gave Sulwesi his name. She could have asked his auntie to give him a proper name, or she could have given him an English name; but no, she would make up what she thought was a nice Indian sounding name.

If it was Indian at all, it would probably be a girl's name. It would be quite a nice name for a girl.

There's an island in Indonesia called Sulawesi. Maybe that's where Mrs Adams got the name, maybe subconsciously. The island used to be called Celebes – at least by Western atlas publishers. Celebes – Sulawesi. Different attempts by Angrezi to pronounce the same word? At least his name is pronounceable, by Indians or by Angrezi.

Mrs Adams could have asked their auntie to look after them too, and they'd have grown up like their cousins. But their father apparently wasn't on speaking terms with their mother's family, and he'd asked Mrs Adams to look after them, so she did. No real thought for them – her first concern was about the promise she'd made to their father. Perhaps she thought he'd check up on her, or perhaps she thought that God was watching her carefully and was more concerned with the letter of her promise than the spirit of thoughtfulness and kindness to the children.

She had no real thought for them – in one sense. In another sense, she couldn't have been kinder. When they were little, they really were treated as part of the family. Sulwesi shared a room with David, and Prema shared a room with Susan. They were just like brothers and sisters.

Then they all went to school together in the little school in the church in the village. The teacher, Pastor Samson, tried his best to treat them all the same. None of them realized until much later that it was more than he could manage to treat the Adams children the same as he treated all the other children from the village. It was just the way things were. In Pastor Samson's mind, Prema and Sulwesi came somewhere in between the English children and the Indians. At that stage of their lives they were closer to David and Susan than they were to the other Indian children.

At home, Dr Adams gave the four of them extra lessons. All four did exactly the same stuff. They learnt all kinds of geography and English history and grammar that no one else in the village was doing. Their spelling and the breadth of their vocabulary mattered; and of course the conversation in the home was quite different from everyone else's, but they didn't realize that until years later. At school they were the four star pupils, but there was never any sign of ill feeling. It was just the way things were. Pastor Samson, himself Indian but raised in a missionary household, taught everything in English, with Hindi just another subject. Their first language was English, but for the other children it was an extra hurdle.

A lady, Muni her name was, used to come up from the village to cook and clean for the Adamses, and sometimes look after the children if Mrs Adams was out or busy. The four children learnt Hindi from Muni when they were little, and looking back Sulwesi thinks she knew it was going to be more important for him and Prema than for the other two, or perhaps she just loved them a little more. Sulwesi and Prema certainly got better at Hindi than Susan and David did. But Muni was illiterate, and it was Dr Adams who taught them Hindi writing and grammar, long before Pastor Samson started on it at school. David and Susan were just as good at written Hindi as Prema and Sulwesi were, but in speech they always sounded like English kids talking Hindi, and Sulwesi thinks he and Prema never did.

The first time Sulwesi and Prema realized that they were not really part of the family was when they all went to Mussoorie to look at the boarding school. David and Susan were going to go there – and Sulwesi and Prema weren't. You couldn't really blame the Adamses: the Mission Society was paying the fees, and the Mission Society didn't accept Sulwesi and Prema as their children. The fees were too much for the

Adamses to pay out of their own pocket – they wouldn't have sent David and Susan if the Mission Society hadn't been paying. And why should the local church spend a large part of its meagre income sending Sulwesi and Prema to boarding school? Why them rather than any of the other Indian kids?

The final blow came when the Adamses had to go back to England. Mr Adams was too sick to stay in India. The Indian immigration rules had changed, and there wasn't going to be another English missionary to replace him. The Indian staff were going to have to carry on the work without support from England – not even any money.

Sulwesi and Prema had never been properly adopted. I don't know if it would have been any different if they had been adopted. They were Indian citizens, and there was no way they were going to be allowed to go to England.

Perhaps they'd have been misfits in England. They didn't feel much different from David and Susan, but by then those two had had four years in a posh boarding school, while Sulwesi and Prema had carried on in the local school system. They certainly felt like misfits among their Indian peers, but they were probably more Indian than English by then. After David and Susan went to boarding school they were left much more to their own devices, and got to know their real relatives properly for the first time.

It was only after the Adamses left that Sulwesi and Prema discovered that the Adamses had been paying fees for them at the local school. All the other kids who passed their exams were getting their fees paid by the Government under a tribal support scheme; but they weren't tribal – not so far as the authorities were concerned. Their parents were English and therefore not tribal; more to the point, they were regarded as rich kids. When the Adamses left they felt like orphans. Who was going to pay their fees now?

Auntie sorted that one out. She just filled the forms in for them as Prema and Suleman, with her own surname instead of Adams, and that was that. Their headmaster knew, but he also knew why. After that, everyone called Sulwesi Suleman for years, which he was quite happy about because it saved a lot of explaining, but he still felt like Sulwesi inside.

They'd had a good start in their education, of course, so they did well. They passed all their exams and got every scholarship that was going, and they've both ended up in good posts. Sulwesi's in Delhi now and Prema's in Bhopal, and they see each other whenever they can, and write to each other a lot. They keep hoping Prema will be able to get a transfer to Delhi but there never seems to be a chance. Both of them miss their Auntie and their cousins a great deal. They only manage to see them once a year.

For a long time they missed the Adamses too. David and Susan had promised they'd write to them, but they never did, and Prema and Sulwesi didn't even have their address. Dr Adams sent them Christmas cards for years, but he never thought of giving them his address. The first few times he wrote a few lines of family news, but then it was just a card, and then it stopped coming altogether – or maybe Auntie started hiding them and pretending they hadn't come, because she knew how much they always upset Sulwesi and Prema.

Sulwesi wondered what would happen if he was too sick to stay in India, or Prema was. It was a purely rhetorical question, of course: what happens to anyone who's too sick for the available health service to cope with?

I promised to try to trace the Adamses for Sulwesi. He probably thought that nothing would come of it, but I'm not like that. I did manage to trace them.

When I found them, I wasn't sure whether to tell him their news, but decided that however badly it might affect him and his sister, I'd better keep to my word. I didn't know whether that was the right decision, but it's what I did.

The easiest way to tell the story is to copy part of my letter to him:

The Adamses were in a car crash five years ago, and David was killed. Dr Adams has been in a wheelchair ever since, but Susan and Mrs Adams weren't seriously hurt. Dr Adams has kept on sending you Christmas cards, so presumably Auntie has been hiding them. He is old and frail now. His mind is still sharp, but Mrs Adams isn't all there at all. How they manage at all is a miracle: he's her brains, and she's his feet.

Dr Adams never managed to get a job after they came back to England, so they've not been well off at all. Mrs Adams did a cleaning job for a few years, and then she worked as a school dinner lady until she got too confused to cope. David started at University but dropped out. He did a couple of dead-end jobs, then he was training as an electrician until he was killed. Susan went to University and got a degree, and now she's married and has two small children.

Dr Adams was very pleased to hear how well you two are doing. I gave him your address in Delhi so that he could avoid the Auntie trap, but he was very unsure about whether it would be a good thing to write to you, after so long, or not. Like I say, he was very pleased to hear how you were doing, but he'd made a decision when they left that it would be fairer to you two not to let you have their address, and force you to find your own way. He knew you'd have to anyway, and he thought it would be better for you not to have an illusory lifeline.

I don't know how to put this, but he still seems to think the same way a bit. He asked me not to give you his address, and let him make his own mind up.

It seems to me that you have more to offer him than vice versa these days, but that's really equally illusory. He can no more go to live in India again than you could have come to England, and even though you're well off in India, you can't send him money. Even if you could, a lot of rupees doesn't come to many pounds and would go nowhere in England at English prices.

I gave Sulwesi my own address. It was a while before he replied. Amongst other things he wrote was this:

Auntie was funny. After all those years of pretending not to have had any post from the Adamses, and without me saying anything, she told us this year that Dr Adams hadn't sent a card – and went and got the old ones. She'd kept them all. She thought that perhaps Dr Adams had died, and I told her about you, and all the news. She cried when she heard about David and Dr Adams.

What upset her most, though, was the fact that in England, Dr and Mrs Adams are obviously nobody special at all.

We've been corresponding ever since, and we've met in Delhi again a couple of times. A quite charming young man, now with an equally charming young wife.

Dr Adams died a couple of years later, and Mrs Adams went to live with Susan and her family. Susan found my address in Dr Adams's papers and wrote to me to let me know. I gave Susan Sulwesi's address and she wrote to Sulwesi too, and asked him to tell Prema – as if she needed to tell him! Sulwesi told me that it was strange to read Susan's letter, and it made him feel very peculiar. He said that her handwriting was just the same as it used to be, but he could tell that her way of thinking had changed completely. At long last, she sent him her address.

Nowadays apparently the Christmas cards go both ways, with little bits of news. Sulwesi wonders if he and Prema will ever see Susan again – to quote one of his letters to me, 'Changed though she is, she still seems a very nice person.'

I've never met Susan myself – I met Dr and Mrs Adams just once.

(Also published in *The Reminiscences of Penny Lane*.)

Odour of Elder Blossom

Harry

I used to sit behind her at school
She was pale with a pigtail
I used to count her vertebrae,
Numbered the lines of the darn
In her well-worn dress,
She was thin, undernourished.

She asked me one day
Would I go for a walk with her?
Grandma Moran said to say no,
'She's far too bold, I tell ye,
I know the Callahans.
You'll be giving her a wide berth now.
Heavens above! You're no more than twelve.'
But how could I refuse.

By the waterside we wandered
Where the elder blossom hung heavy.
'Til we came to the weir where we turned
And walked in innocence while she told me
Things she could tell to no one else.
There was no one else she would trust.

'Mi dad's in the army.
Away in the war. Mam's upset,
'cause we've got no money'.

Ten years later when I met her again
She didn't know me nor anyone else,
Her eyes, black tarns where only sorrows lived,
Gazed only into an empty pram.
Ah, You mean Lizzie Garret
Lizzie Callahan that was.
Lost her baby. Lost her mind.
So they told me when I enquired.
But I remember Lizzie Callahan
And sweet elder blossom.

The Burning Window

John

Buddhaven Manor – now a corporate retreat in the Westmorland countryside – has a history dating back to the time of Henry the Eighth. Built by Sir James Nancekieval within the grounds of the recently destroyed Heymanceaux Monastery – the house reflected the family's growing influence in the North west of England.

Whilst the front of the house was extensively renovated in the 18th Century to reflect the classical tastes of the time, the sides and rear still have many of their original tudor features.

One window – on the eastern side of the property has – unusually – its own name, and a certain amount of unusual history; this is the burning window.

The eldest grandson of Sir James was a man named Anthony Nancekieval, and was known in the county as a fervent – some said fanatical – Christian of the puritan persuasion. He was known to have corresponded with Matthew Hopkins on the matter of identifying and prosecuting witches. This fanaticism set him at odds with the local residents, and especially the priest of the nearby church of St Mungos, The Reverend Whittle.

When a local woman was accused of Witchcraft, the Priest refused to believe she was guilty, even to the point of speaking in her favour at her trial – and in fact secured her release. This incensed Nancekieval who decided to take matters into his own hands. with the aid of some of his servants he took the woman to his house and arranged for her to be burned for her witchcraft; and for this purpose a pyre was hastily built on the eastern side of the house.

Nancekieval watched the scene from the house, staring through the closest window as the woman was burnt. However before the flame was set to the pyre the woman was reported to have looked up at the window and said: "Thou – who stare with such joy through that window. Let the flames come – I have no fear for my soul. But I swear upon all that is Holy that these flames shall be seen again; to the ruin of thee and thy kin".

Nancekieval was dead within the year, after falling down the house's staircase and breaking his neck. On the very night that he died a servant swore that whilst outside walking on the east side of the house, he had looked up and saw a fiery glow coming from the window where Anthony Nancekieval had watched the burning.

The last of the Nancekieval family – Wilfred – died in 1929, and the house fell into disrepair for the next few decades before being refurbished by a local businessman.

However it was said by the family that flames seen in the burning window was a sure sign of a death in the Nancekieval family. Wilfred was reported as saying that he knew when his son Peter had been killed during the Great War through this.

Wilfred's grandfather had boarded up the window in 1878, saying that "A rational man does not fear such absurdities." However after experiencing a series what he described as "horrific nightmares of falling," he allowed the window to be unbarred; and was said to have never experienced those dreams again.

La Vague (the Wave)

Meryem

It is three in the morning. I do not sleep. I hear the sound of the sea, the waves crashing against the cliffs with a sigh, gnawing at the uncaring stones with their tears. I always loved the sound of the sea, this companion in solitude. The regular swoosh, with the small arrhythmias of a live thing.

When I was a child, I could spend hours watching for the seventh wave, the one that was bigger than the others. But to find the seventh wave, the problem is to know the first. For when a seventh wave is smaller than the previous one, it is that it was not the seventh? Which then? This is the arbitrariness of beginnings. There was one day a first wave and seventh wave, stronger than the others.

Probably no one was there to see. No, nothing. The first wave took place before the first heartbeat of the first paramecium. The first wave, no one can tell, because no one knows that the second wave will come, nor the third, nor the forty-ninth.

Yet one day, someone said "the seventh wave is always stronger than the others." That someone had watched the sea for long enough to work out the count of the waves.

I did not know how he did it. I was too young to know the laws of series. I had not thought to take a wave, and then note the sizes of the next seven waves, to identify this starting point that would have taken me back to the origin of the world. But someone had done it. Someone who knew the sea well enough, who had so studied the sea that he could say without error that, in any weather, at high tide, at low tide, in calm or storm, the seventh wave is the strongest.

There were half-waves, too, the little pieces of which came together as waves arriving at the beach, or on the contrary, the waves were breaking into two waves on a rock. How was it counted? The seventh wave – was it seventh when it was forming, far off, away from my sight, as impossible to see and recognize as that first wave before the first paramecium? Was it seventh when I saw it appear in my sight, ten meters from the shore, at that place where I was not allowed to go swimming, because I was too small – even the *first* wave could have drowned such a waif – or was it seventh at the time when it expired in foam on the wet sand?

I was seven, and looking for the essence of the world in the seventh wave.

Bunker I

Stephen

Eleven thirty at night, Berrenton Town Hall. Before we go inside let's consider the building itself for a moment. The original town hall had been an industrial revolution gothic epic, far grander than the small town of Berrenton really deserved. Some shady dealing in the sixties led to it being sold and demolished much to the anger of the town's residents. The mayor at the time retired in disgrace but was later quietly placed on the honours list. The new building is, well, horrendous. Essentially three intersecting concrete blocks in the classic sixties council style. Which is to say none.

Let's take a look inside. First up we have Howard. Howard is the last remaining security guard, having survived the cull. Where previously he had been a member of a team of ten he is now the only nightman left. The building stands empty at weekends. Howard is aware how precarious his position is but is confident he won't be sacked and replaced with a security system just yet. It would of course be too expensive, but Howard has other reasons for his confidence. He is currently standing in a camera blindspot, smoking a rollie while leaning against a no smoking sign. He has done this on purpose which should tell you a lot about Howard.

Stubbing out his fag Howard returns to his rounds. As he turns a corner he removes some keys from his pocket and begins jingling them loudly as he whistles a jaunty tune. He reaches the end of the corridor and stops at a lit office. He takes a moment to compose himself and then enters.

Inside we have Councillor Desmond Hayne, chief deputy secretary to the deputy mayor. And his assistant, Mary Halliwell. Now, you had a mental image of Desmond when you read his name and title and he pretty much matches it. While he claims to his wife that he regularly attends the gym, a quick look at his waistline dispels this fantasy. Desmond likes power, but has reached the limit of what is attainable to someone of his limited imagination. He's very close to a comb over. Mary on the other hand is a lot brighter. And a lot younger. And a lot more likely to rise through the ranks, if only because of her willingness to indulge tired old men's fantasies to get her own way. She's currently trapped and she knows it. Its only a matter of time before Desmond realises that what he really has over her is blackmail material. Fortunately he thus far is lost in a fantasy that is all too common among middle age executive types.

The couple look up from either side of a large table. Desmond is looking red and a little sweaty but Mary is as demure as it's possible to be. Howard glances down at the waste paper bin and pretends not to notice the pair of knickers in it.

HOWARD – Working late again I see?

DESMOND – Yes, yes, well, you know me.

Howard smiles and nods. He glances at Mary who smiles sweetly and gives him a quick nod back.

HOWARD – Yes sir, well you know where I am if you need me.

And with another nod at the room's occupants he departs whistling more quietly to himself, his job secure for a while longer at least.

So that's three people and it's now approaching midnight so let's look at the fourth person in the building. Colin. Colin is a cleaner. He too survived the cull, although in his case this is possibly due to his willingness to work beyond his paid hours. But then, Colin has very good reasons for needing to keep the job. He needs access to the Town Hall. Some time ago Colin was made homeless and has since then been living in the town hall basement. Nobody is aware of this, yet.

He is currently leaning on a mop and staring admiringly at a newly clean corridor. Which Howard then walks down. The two regard each other with a hint of distaste. Colin because no cleaner likes it when someone walks over a wet floor and Howard because Colin is the scum of the earth.

HOWARD – Are you not done yet?

COLIN – Was just about to head back to the cupboard and get off.

HOWARD – Well hurry up, you were supposed to be out of here an hour ago.

Colin nods and picks up his bucket. As Howard returns to the security office Colin knows how much time he has. He returns to the cleaning cupboard and stows his gear. He dumps his council smock in his cubby hole and heads for the exit. When he gets there he opens the door with his security pass, which will be duly noted in the security room and shuts it again with him still inside. He then moves swiftly to the stair well and heads down into the depths of the building.

After a few twists and turns he reaches a locked storage cupboard. This he unlocks and slips into. Once inside he walks casually to an overlarge filing cabinet and reaches behind it. A switch is flicked. The cabinet slowly and smoothly slides aside to reveal a bank vault style door that is itself opening. Colin wanders through into a well lit battleship grey corridor. He follows the corridor until he enters a large hall. On the wall are the words 'Regional Emergency Command Centre'

Colin had discovered the bunker some time ago. It had at first been a curiosity as he wandered the vastness of it. Floor after floor, corridor after corridor. The bunker had been designed in the sixties but only finished in the seventies. It had then been upgraded a little in the eighties but since then it had been mothballed and all but forgotten.

But it was the hydroponics unit that had originally taken his interest and it is there that he heads to now. At first he had visited only occasionally, but when he had been made homeless he had essentially moved in. Eventually he enters hydroponics unit one. He walks across to a kettle and flicks it on and then walks down the rows of plants murmuring pleasantries to them and checking the odd brown leaf. When the kettle boils he returns and makes himself a brew as he gazes fondly at the room filled with happy, healthy, extra large marijuana plants. As he sips his drink he smiles to himself and gives a long, deeply felt sigh of relief.

We will leave him there for the moment, happily oblivious to the world above him. Which is a shame because he had often fantasized about the events that are about to occur.

Howard sits in his security office, also sipping a beverage. He is more than a little shocked when red lights start flashing and a siren goes off. He hadn't been aware that such a siren even existed. Glancing at the cameras he notices that Desmond and Mary have stepped out into the corridor and are looking at the lights with a similar level of confusion. They head for the main entrance as Howard attempts to work out where the off switch is. The siren begins to alternate with the plum tomes of a BBC announcer.

ALERT – Emergency, emergency. For your own safety please head to the shelter provided.

HOWARD – What fucking shelter??

He jumps up from his seat and heads to the main exit. He gets there just as Desmond and Mary arrive.

DESMOND – What the fuck is going on?

HOWARD – How the hell should I know?

DESMOND – It's a siren, surely that's your bloody job?

HOWARD – Fire alarm, burglar alarm sure, but what the hell is this?

They are both shouting despite the fact that the siren isn't actually all that loud.

Mary returns from having tried the main door.

MARY – It's locked, Des?

Desmond frowns and heads for the door. He scans his security pass over the receiver but nothing happens. He tries again. Nothing. He is barged out of the way by Howard who tries his security pass. Also nothing.

ALERT – Emergency, emergency. T minus 4 minutes to impact.

The three council workers look at each other.

Desmond takes the lead.

DESMOND – To the elevator!

Howard looks at him but doesn't move.

DESMOND – Downstairs, there's an old shelter from the cold war.

MARY – Really?

DESMOND – Yes really, what shelter do you think he means?

Mary and Howard allow Desmond to lead them to the elevator and they head down. Once at the bottom of the elevator shaft Desmond opens a panel on the wall.

DESMOND – Eric brought me down here when I started years ago. Huge great boondoggle at the time.

He presses down on a button with one hand and then jabs the button for the ninth floor three times. The lift judders slightly and then descends a further floor. Both Mary and Howard stare open mouthed at him.

ALERT – Emergency, emergency. T minus two minutes to impact.

The doors to the elevator open to reveal a waiting room with a large vault like door at the far end. Lights flick on as they enter the room and the door slowly begins to swing open. The three of them run to it but have to wait precious seconds as it opens widely enough for them to get through. Something of a design flaw. Once through Desmond slams the door seal lock down and all three of them watch as the door closes once more. A clock above the door reads twenty years, zero days, zero hours, zero minutes and begins to tick down.

Voices

Clive

"Don't touch me!"
"I've no intention of touching you!"
And I haven't.

But I have, and you didn't tell her that.

WHY WOULD HE? YOU'RE NOT IN CONTROL.

But I might be in a minute!

I HOPE NOT.

"You seemed to, a moment ago."
"I'm sorry, I don't know what came over me."

Liar! You know damn well what came over you.

Indeed I do, but it's not something I can explain, is it? Anyway, I'm in full control now, and I intend to stay that way. Somehow.

IT'S TWO TO ONE. I'LL DO MY BEST TO HELP. BUT HE'S STRONG.

I know that. But this is important.
Concentrate on the driving. It helps to be concentrating on something, changes of control are less likely, especially if it's something potentially hazardous one's concentrating on. I just hope we don't have to stop again.
She's nodding off again.

Darkness, wet road, no light anywhere except our headlights. Raindrops caught in the light, and not much else to see, because the wet road surface reflects the light away from us not back in our direction.

Can't think of Viv without remembering her last moments. I don't want to think of her last moments, I want to think of all the happy times. But the memory of her lying there dying, knowing she was dying, knowing that she was conscious and that she too knew she was dying, always comes to the fore. That, and the memory of the explosion itself.

God, that was close. Going too fast? Maybe, slow down a bit. And stop daydreaming – daydreaming at night? Not nightdreaming. Not dreaming at all. Reminiscing.

Amazing that Ella trusts me enough to sleep. Either that, or she's incredibly tired, which is quite likely I suppose.

Light in the distance behind – a bright flash on the horizon, illuminating half the sky. Lightning? An explosion? I don't know. Couldn't see it properly – only caught a glimpse in the mirrors. Headlights? Could be, I suppose, but awfully bright if so – and just one brief flash?

In restless dreams I walked alone
Narrow streets of cobblestone
'Neath the halo of a street lamp
I turn my collar to the cold and damp
When my eyes were stabbed by the flash of a neon light

Damn – must have dozed off. God, we're headed straight for a wall. Quick – brake, steer hard left, phew. Must stay awake!

Driving, driving, getting away.

How's the petrol? About a third full now – and two five-litre jerry cans in the back. Could do two hundred plus miles, more if I slow down. What's the chance of getting some more? Steal some? And get shot? No thanks.

Too much water on the road here – sliding, slewing, correct the skid, thank goodness that worked. Slow down a bit.

"Have you told your wife?"

Ah. She's awake again.

"I shan't tell her anything unless there's something to tell her."

"Isn't there anything to tell her?"

"I don't know. Is there?"

"What would it have to be to make you think there was something to tell her?"

"Well, if you and I decided we wanted to get a place together, have kids, that sort of thing."

"Do you think that's likely?"

"I don't know. Depends on two things, I suppose. Do you like me that much? Do I like you that much? There's an awful lot you don't know about me. I don't really know all that much about you, either."

Silence for a mile or two – apart from the swoosh of the wipers and the noise of the car speeding along the wet road. Engine, tyres, spray.

Then I break the silence. "How much do you like me?"

"I like you a lot. How much do you like me?"

"I like you a lot, too. But do I like you that much? I don't know you well enough yet to know. You don't know me well enough to know yet, either."

"How often does this happen to you?"

"Never happened before."

"When did you know it was happening?"

"The realization dawned on me gradually, but I was aware of something from the moment I first met you."

"Same here."

She's changed her tune since she was telling you not to touch her. You should ask her about that.

I'm not sure I should, and since it's still me in control, I'm not saying anything.

Silence again for a while. A car, going in the opposite direction – the first we've seen in ages.

"I'm sorry I was a bit short with you earlier on."

"No call to be sorry. I'm sorry if I scared you a bit."

"I shouldn't have been scared. Half the time I want you to touch me anyway."

"Half the time I know that, and half the time I'm not sure. Half the time I don't know what I want myself."

Silence, and a safe distance between us.

Driving, driving, getting away.

Snores.

He really doesn't know what he wants, does he?

NO, HE REALLY DOESN'T. EVERYONE KNOWS WHAT YOU WANT.

What about you?

I WANT THE BEST FOR EVERYONE. I DON'T ALWAYS KNOW WHAT THAT IS.

Do I get any say in this?

YOU CERTAINLY DO. YOU'RE IN CONTROL.

Yeah. And I'm trying to drive.

You could put your arm round her shoulder quite easily.

Yeah. And crash the car. Good plan.

Staring into the darkness. Raining harder now – and a bit of sleet, by the looks of it. Blue flashing lights in the distance ahead. I wonder if anyone is looking for us? I wish I knew the area.

Chances are very strong that it's nothing to do with us.

A sign for a minor road on the left. I hope it connects through to somewhere, and avoids whatever it is going on up ahead. Take the corner as fast as I safely can. Her head lolls onto my shoulder, and stays there.

That's nice.

It is. But don't get too excited.

I'm not. This road needs some concentration to take at any speed in the dark and wet.

Trees overhanging the road from both sides, making a sort of tunnel. Hope we get a reasonable right turn before too long, and that it won't bring us back onto the main road too soon.

What are you afraid of? What's the worst that can happen? She's in two minds as much as we are, and I'm not thinking of raping her.

Two minds? I make it three.

Yeah. At least. Anyone else around here at the moment?

If she's in two minds now, even if she and I are both in the same mood at the same time sometimes, how long will it last? Half the time one of us will want us to be together, and the other won't.

"I'm sorry, I must have dozed off."

"That's all right. You need some sleep."

"You know, it's no good. Half the time one of us or the other will want us to be together when the other doesn't."

"That's incredible. That's exactly what I was thinking a moment before you woke up."

> *Yeah. And it's the story of human life. Get a grip. Don't waste your life. A quarter of the time we'll both want to be apart, and a quarter we'll both want to be together. That quarter outweighs all the other three quarters easily.*

> *MAYBE. BUT I WANT TO GET TO KNOW HER BETTER FIRST.*

I thought you were on my side.

> *I AM. BUT HE'S GOT A POINT.*

I know. But like she said, "it's no good."
Not to worry, I'm still firmly in control.

> *Yeah, but how long for? Down this side road, there must be somewhere quiet we can stop.*

I'm not stopping. What I want is a route to rejoin the main road somewhere beyond those blue lights.

A turning on the right – but it's too narrow, and not signposted. Doesn't look as though it goes anywhere, we could get hopelessly lost. It might even dump us back on the main road too soon. Keep straight on.

Open country now, climbing into the hills. Rain stopping. Clouds beginning to break up. Moonlight!

"Do slow down a bit. Look – there's a place we could stop for few minutes – that boarded-up old place at the top of the hill must have somewhere to pull off."

Ha. What did I tell you?

Oh Gawd. Now what do I do?
"I'm not sure that's such a good idea."
Driving, driving, getting away.
"I need a wee."

HA. WHAT WAS THAT YOU TOLD ME?

"Ah. Okay. There's no traffic about. We can stop anywhere. There's a place for you to disappear for a minute just there."

Should I turn the engine off? Probably better to leave it running, she won't be long. Lights off. World looks much better with just the moonlight. Those are big piles of cloud up in the north, though. Could easily be snow before long.

Door slamming, not very hard though. She's back.
"You were nodding off! Are you fit to be driving?"
"I'll be okay for quite a while yet."
"I'm sorry I can't drive."
"You're even more tired than I am anyway. I'll be okay."
"Are you sure? If we put the back seats down, there'll be just about room for us to lie down in the

back. Find somewhere safe to park, and we can sleep for a while."

"If I turn the engine off, it'll be freezing in here pretty quick."

"We'll be okay if we snuggle up close."

Ha. What did I tell you?

She didn't need a wee at all, you know. That was just to make you stop, and a way to pretend, when you'd rebuffed her, that she hadn't been making advances.

Maybe. Who knows?

Oh Gawd.

"I think we'd still freeze to death in our sleep."

That's probably the truth, too. Even if I have got other reasons for saying it.

Driving, driving, getting away.

"PTSD doesn't only happen in the military." "PTSD?" "Post-traumatic stress disorder." "Give it a label, that'll cure me." "Will he recover?" "Life'll never be the same again."

Damn fool doctor. Life was never the same before, either, I've always been like this. I wouldn't want to be any other way anyway, this is who I am. And stop reminiscing, you old fool – you'll crash the car.

That wouldn't be such a bad way to go, all in all.

Better to freeze in your sleep than crash the car.

Better not to do either. Not fair to Ella. Concentrate on the driving.

The Mystery of Peter Mither

John

Many nursery rhymes and children's street chants are known to be little historical snippets that have lost their original meaning over time. Many believe that "Ring a Ring a Roses" refers to the Great Plague of the 16th Century; and so on.

However, many are at a loss to explain one of the now-extinct London chants; or rather they are at a loss as to how and even why it survived for so long.

Although not heard for at least 150 years, the children inhabiting the area surrounding the Church of St Winnifrith o' the Wall had a very particular chant that was all their own:

Peter Mither, Peter Mither
Sell your red tomatoes hither
Tom Tayro, Tom Tayro,
Tom bully for you!

Charles Dickens makes a reference to this chant in a piece he wrote for the Illustrated London News in 1852, noting that it is one of the many chants of its kind that just seem to refer to some eccentric character from the local area's past.

In 1934, as part of the extension of the Jubilee line, workmen tunnelling near the Church of St Winnifrith o' the Wall made the unexpected discovery of a hitherto unknown Roman underground structure. It appeared to be some sort of temple, and the faded mural (now recognised as being one of the best preserved in northern Europe) depicting a youth stabbing a bull made it clear that this was a Temple to the God Mithras. As a god beloved of soldiers, temples to Mithras – always underground – could be found all over the empire, wherever the legions went; and the church was well within the boundaries of the Roman city of Londinium.

The discovery caused a brief flurry of interest in the area around the Church of St Winnifrith, especially as it was not particularly close to the already known location of Londinium's soldier's quarters.

However, a carving discovered on one of the walls put a much darker complexion on the situation: *Pater Mithrae magnum, sanguinem per vitulum oephi* (Great Father Mithras, blood for the bull).

Although in the vast majority of cases, known practices of the Cult of Mithras involved the sacrifice of a bull; a particularly unsavoury sect practiced cannibalism. Temples of this sect were mostly found in the eastern Mediterranean, in Anatolia (Turkey) and the Aegean islands. It called itself the Blood of the Bull. The inscription on the wall referred to the oath made by the cultists at the point that the sacrificial victim of the cult was ritually killed, dismembered and eaten.

So where does Peter Mither feature in this story? When Translated into Greek, the inscription on the wall becomes *O patéras tou Míthra, tou aímatos gia ton távro*.

If Peter Mither was Father Mithras, how did this chant survive for so long, and why would it even be remembered in the first place? More perplexing still, the chant only comes close to matching the Greek translation rather than the actual Latin inscription. Nowhere in the shrine is the Greek text found.

Many think that there is still a mystery to uncover in the area of the Church of St Winnifrith o' the Wall.

Something Bad

Aidan

He didn't want her to die. He didn't want the girl to die. Not to die. He loved her. And he wanted her to love him. That was all. But she didn't. He could tell she didn't. Didn't love him. He didn't know why. He loved her. He didn't mean for her to die. He didn't know, that was all. Why she didn't. Why she couldn't. Why she.

*

It was cold standing out every night by the river, but he didn't mind. He'd feel the dew start to settle, the mist begin to form among the reeds. But he had that bright rectangle of light, her kitchen window, to absorb him, to draw all his attention, his hope and intuition, and to keep him warm, or at least keep him from noticing, or minding, the chill. So he watched. To see her. See her moving. Among the cupboards. The coffee jar. The cooker. Busying herself, sometimes for the longest time, at the cooker, those rapid movements to get things from the shelves, tip things, pour things, cut things. With the kitchen knives. The one she chopped down with, the one she sawed with in quick short movements, the one she drew back and forth in a longer, slower rhythm, the one she used as if she was carving something in wood.

He never saw the knives, or almost never, but he knew each one by its movement, which drawer they came from; though the drawer itself was below his line of sight, he knew just how much she had to turn, how far she had to bend. He liked it best when she reached up for something off the high shelves, because then. He liked the shape she made.

Or when she stood at the sink washing dishes and he saw the way the bubbles clung to the skin of her arms. Then she faced him, he could see her buttons and the delicate chain at her neck, and sometimes she'd look straight at him but not knowing he was there looking back and it made him feel quite funny. Maybe he liked it. Maybe he didn't. Maybe it was the best time of all, or the worst, it was that funny feeling you couldn't tell.

And there was a time she cut herself, just a little cut with the small sharp chopping-downwards knife, but he saw her blood, and her sucking the bleeding finger, and running it under the tap, and then her blood again, and she was facing right towards him and he felt the excitement of her pain, even though it wasn't really very much pain. He didn't want her to have any more pain than that.

And he didn't want the man there. Most times he could forget the man. He was just a dimly understood presence beyond the door, like the distant flicker sometimes of a television. But sometimes he stood waiting for her to come and the man came instead to take something from the fridge or make coffee. But the man didn't matter and he never stayed long. Some nights he never came at all. Just one time he came behind her at the sink, put his hand round her and his mouth on her hair, and then. And then. And then the water was cold and the river-mud felt unpleasant and the reeds nasty and.

And after that he didn't go back for several weeks. He went to the pub instead and drank on his own in a corner until a night he got in a fight, got a swollen lip and a cut eyebrow, and after that he stayed in his room nights until eventually he had to see her again.

She'd got her hair cut in the meantime and at first it just didn't seem right, but he made himself keep watching and soon it was normal, like how he felt it must be to have old friends and see them again after a time. And that was the first time he started to wonder what her name was. But pretty soon he knew, he understood, that it would spoil something if she had a name. If she was Jane, or Sandra, or Tracey she would be just another Jane, Sandra or Tracey. But she wasn't. She was She. And actually he liked her hair shorter, he could imagine the scissors snipping around her neck and the secret place just behind her ears, and the bristly feeling of the new-cut ends close against her skin, though they probably weren't that new-cut now already, and he had liked the way it had fallen across her shoulders before, and the way it swung when she turned, and those moments he could suddenly see her face when she tucked her hair behind her ear, a moment of revealing like. Like. Like when.

And it was after then that he saw the little girl. For the first time.

Funny that he had managed not to know about her. Till then. Till the evening she dashed away from her dishes, hardly pausing to wipe her hands, and then a light went on behind a pink curtain upstairs, and he wondered. And thought. And then there was the girl, surprising him, looking out. And that's when it all changed.

*

Taking the girl should have been planned. He should have thought about how he was going to do it, and when. Where he would take her. How he would keep her hidden. What they would do together to pass the time, and how much time it would be. How he would feed her. Him too. It ought to have all been carefully thought out, like a commando raid or a bank robbery. He could have done it. He could have.

But if he stopped to ask how, he would have asked himself why as well, and then he wouldn't have done it.

No. It wasn't like that. Taking the girl wasn't something he planned. It wasn't something he did. It was something that happened to him.

For one thing it happened in daylight. He'd never done anything bad in daylight before. In fact he'd never really done anything bad before. Not really bad. Except that once with that baby bird he found by the river, and that didn't count, he'd still been at school then, and anyway he didn't enjoy it, it was just something he had to do, something you were supposed to do when you were 13. That was different anyway. Anyway.

Watching wasn't bad. It didn't hurt anyone. Just standing outside watching her didn't hurt. It was like watching television, the people in the television don't know you're there, and wouldn't care if they did. Knowing she was real was good, though, really there, not like on television, and knowing she didn't know he was there. Watching. It was something private. Something between them, but it was just his, not hers. With the girl it was different.

She came with him quite happily at first, that was how it happened. By the river, on the bus. Only on the bus she started to get anxious, wanted to know where they were going, and then he got anxious too and wanted to know too. But he didn't know.

The bus was going in to town. There were people, but there would be more people in town. He might lose her, or worse she might start making a fuss and give him away. And it was when he thought that he began to think he was doing something bad. And his anxiety started to feel more like panic.

They would get off at the next stop, on the bridge near the docks. Not many people there, and it might seem like an adventure. To her. And to him. A hand round her wrist was all it took to get her off the bus with him. Outside the stuffy confines of the bus he began to feel better at once. In control. Or something like. Able to breathe. Able to think.

*

The old warehouse seemed like a good idea at first. It was quiet and totally private. It was only a short walk from the shops in town but there was no risk of anyone intruding and he was pretty sure he could come and go without being seen. Pretty sure. It was like he'd had the idea all along, and that was why they'd had to get off at the bridge. In control.

He had to force a way in through an old door that had been nailed up years ago, and that was when the girl started to struggle. Holding on to her with one hand, he tried to lever the door open with a length of wood he picked up in the other, but he found it difficult and as he applied himself more to the door she wriggled free of his grasp. For a moment they both stood and stared at each other, a moment of revelation and doubt, then she began to run.

If she got to the corner of the building there was a real chance she would be seen by someone walking by the old dock or on the bridge. If she screamed even now someone might hear. For the first time he felt fear. He took two or three strides, realised he might not catch her before she got to the corner, and as if instinctively threw the piece of wood he had been holding. It caught her on the back of the legs, sending her sprawling to the ground, which was old broken concrete littered with bits of brick, and glass, and rusty metal, and with weeds growing through. She cut her hand and her knee as she fell. He reached her just as she began to cry out, and in panic he clapped a hand over her mouth. He picked her up and held her tightly to him while she squirmed and kicked and bit his hand. If someone came round the corner now. If someone heard her. If she got away. She bit into the fleshy base of his thumb, drawing blood, and in the second her mouth was free he felt, rather than heard, her draw breath to scream. He butted her with his forehead, a little too hard, the back of her head cracked against the dirty brick wall of the warehouse and she went limp in his arms.

Oh God. Oh no. He'd hurt her. He never meant to hurt her. He'd never hurt anybody. It was just. It was just. She was going to scream, that's all.

It was all right. She was breathing. She wasn't dead or anything. He put his hand gently to the back of her head, but there wasn't any blood. It was all right. He could breathe again. He hadn't touched her hair before. It was so soft. He'd never touched anyone's hair. Not a girl's. Nobody's except his own, and then. Hers was so soft and warm and lovely.

He carried her gently to the door. He still had to break a way in, without dropping her or hurting her. He cradled her still limp form high on his chest, lifted his leg and gave the door the hardest kick he dared with the sole of his boot. At the fourth or fifth kick he felt something crack, and with the next one some of the wood of the door broke away enough for him to bend low, still carrying the girl, and wriggle his way in.

It was dark inside, a dim world of spiders and weeds. Rats probably. It smelt dusty. Vaguely industrial. Oily somehow, like a garden fence in summer. It smelt of brick dust and old wood. It smelt old, forgotten. Beneath all that it smelt like Weetabix.

As his eyes grew accustomed he saw he was in a huge room, lit by the hole he had just broken in through and by a few other odd chinks or cracks in the walls. Thin beams picked out dusty air like a distant view of searchlights in a war film. The pitted floor was covered in pale dust like flour. The wooden roof was held up by upright beams and props like in a mine. There were some ropes hanging down. A few empty sacks lay around, and there were some that looked full of something propped against one or two of the upright posts. Overhead an opening into an upper floor showed up as a square of a slightly different shade of gloom. A stairway that was almost a ladder, like a ship's companionway, led up to it.

He hoisted the girl onto his shoulder, her head and arms hanging down behind him, her legs sticking out a little awkwardly in front, and began to climb. Once he was sure the steps were sound, it was easy. They went up into another room, or open space, exactly like the first, only the floor was wooden and if anything more thickly carpeted with dust. The Weetabix smell was a little stronger.

The floor above was the same, and the one above that. Up here, though, there were a few windows, small, grimed and cobwebbed over, but still letting in a bit of light. The atmosphere was thick, warm and heady. He decided to go right to the top.

Six floors up it was. The ceiling was lower than in the other rooms and not bare boards but cracked, dirty plaster which sagged badly in several places. There were windows in three of the walls, slightly larger than on the floors below, and two of them were broken which made the air pleasanter to breathe. Several pigeons had got in. There were signs of old nests, and feathers and droppings all over the floor. The white dust was not so thick here, though. Even up here the roots of a few plants had penetrated and hung down inside the walls. Willowherb was growing in through one of the broken windows,

The girl came to, a little groggily, and began to cry. He tried to comfort her by showing her the view from the window, which looked out splendidly over all the rooftops and towerblocks of the town. She wasn't comforted but her wails gradually became short, shallow, rapid sobs. He held her in his arms and gently rocked her, humming a soothing sound low in his throat, his hand caressing her hair. Close by the window you could just hear the sound of traffic far below.

*

She was hungry, she was thirsty, she was scared, most of all she wanted her mummy. He couldn't help everything, but he could get food and drink. He would need some himself too. But how could be leave her securely? There was nowhere he could shut her in, nothing to tie her with. Maybe the ropes he had seen hanging on the floors below?

He had to go backwards down the steps, leaving her whimpering above. No rope he could see on this floor. He would try the level below. Two floors down there was some old rope hanging, part of an old hoist system, but was stiff, as thick as his wrist. He had nothing to cut it with, and anyway it would be impossible to tie.

She hadn't tried to follow him down the steps. Perhaps if he went she would stay there, too scared to go anywhere. She'd been unconscious when he carried her up. She wouldn't know where she was, how she'd got there, or how to get out. The steps might be too big for her, too steep, the drop from top to bottom too great, for her to dare. If she did try to follow him down she would soon find herself in dark, creepy places. He found those big empty dusty rooms a little scary, so a child surely would. Probably if he left her to buy food and drink she'd stay where she was till he got back. Probably.

And if she was gone when he returned? Well then she'd be gone. It would be over. Nothing more for him to worry about. Perhaps that would be best.

Maybe if he went away for a long time? She could just leave. If wouldn't be his fault if she didn't. If he just went away and didn't come back. He wouldn't have to worry about her any more.

Floor by floor he left her, and the responsibility for her, behind. Stepping out at last through the broken door he felt the bright shock of the daylight and the relieving breath of fresh air.

*

He heated a can of beans on the gas ring in his room and ate them on toast. He wanted badly to go out as usual and watch from his usual place at the river's edge, but he knew that tonight that was not a good idea. He wanted everything to be calm and normal. To watch her cutting vegetables, pouring coffee, washing pots. He knew tonight she wouldn't be doing that. He wanted to watch her anyway, but he didn't dare go.

Instead he went to the pub, but he knew as he walked in the door that the atmosphere was not like normal, and he didn't want to stay. So instead of a drink he bought cigarettes and took them home to smoke. For some reason he felt like smoking, though usually he didn't. He had no lighter, but there were the matches he used to light the gas. The beans tin would do for an ashtray. He turned on the television. There, filling his room in a sudden blaze of brilliance, was her face. It wasn't a very recent picture, a grainy family snap of her splashing in a paddling pool, the face blown up too large on the bright screen, but he knew at once it was her. And then there was the mother, looking thinner and wilder than usual, her eyes puffy red and panicky, flicking from side to side as if she was trying to look past the camera while she spoke about her missing daughter. And there, on a caption, they gave her a name. Damn. Damn. She was spoiled for him now. It would never be the same.

The girl must be still in the warehouse or there wouldn't be a news story. Or it would be a happy one, and she'd be there, the mother hugging her with happy tears instead of sad ones. He wanted to smash the television set, but instead he pressed the off switch on the remote control with deliberate calmness and it was as if the walls of his room rushed in suddenly and suffocated him, all light and existence snuffed out in the dying of the light from the screen.

*

He lay awake sweating, aware of his heart, of pounding in his ears, of a metal taste in his mouth, a sick feeling that went right down to his legs. He thought he'd wet himself. Then he thought he might be having a heart attack.

He got up while it was still dark and smoked a cigarette. The drug made his head spin but it was better than he had felt just before. He had to go back to the warehouse, but he wouldn't take the bus. That would mean waiting two or three hours for the first one, and for some reason he felt nervous now about people seeing him, especially on that bus route. The walk along the river would do him good, and it would be light by the time he got there. If he kept to the footpath on the other side of the river he wouldn't have to go past her house, and he wouldn't be fatally tempted to stop and look.

When he got to the outskirts of town there was a newsagent's shop just opening. At first he strode past, knowing what would be on the front of the local paper and not wanting to see. Then he paused and went back, steeling himself to cast just a normal disinterested glance. He even dared himself to pick up a copy and

there they both were, a nursery photo of the girl this
time, the woman almost unbearably hugging the man.
Not, it was not unbearable. She had a name now. She
was no longer who she had been for him. And she and
the man both looked so bleak and grim he felt sorry for
them. Too much emotion, too much time, for the casual
passer-by he had meant to appear. He would have to
buy the paper now, and he did, along with bread, milk,
beans and chocolate. Just a normal man's normal early-
morning shopping. And then, seeing a teddy bear in the
window as he left the shop, he went back in to buy it,
and while he was there he thought of breakfast and not
knowing what she liked he got a selection pack of
different cereals. And then he had to go back a third
time to buy a plastic bowl and spoon, and this time he
thought the man at the counter gave him a strange look,
a bit too long and a bit too thoughtful. He would have
liked to make a joke to laugh off his strange purchases,
but he couldn't think what to say and he had to force
himself to walk casually and calmly out of the shop
with his bags instead of dropping them and running.

*

He expected to find her exactly where he had left
her, and it gave him a jolt to find she wasn't there. A
moment of alarm was followed by a moment of
elation. It was over. And then a surge of fresh alarm,
turning quickly to fear. Where was she? What if she.
What had happened? What was going to happen? Was
she. Had she.

He flung down his shopping bags, spun round
quickly, making cobwebs and bits of pigeons' nests
scatter as he looked into all corners of the room. She

wasn't there. If her feet had made prints in the thick dust, his own had obliterated them. But the windows were no more broken than they had been, so if she had gone it could only have been down the steps. He went down them himself, peering all round in the gloom of the floor below to see if she was there. On the next steps down he half slipped, making the mistake of trying to go down forwards in his hurry. On the next flight he was more careful, taking the steps backwards, one at a time. As he reached the floor he almost trod on her.

She was lying, curled up into a ball, by the foot of the steps. She was covered in dust and dirt. Her lovely hair was very mussed up and filthy. She wasn't moving. Perhaps she had fallen, slipping sideways off the steps in fear or panic, or just because her legs weren't long enough to reach them safely. It was only because she had fallen to one side that he hadn't tripped against her on his way up. It was only because of the darkness and his hurry that he hadn't seen her.

How long had she been lying there? Had she tried to follow him almost at once? Or had nightfall terrified her into trying to find a way out? Maybe daybreak this morning had given her the courage to try. Maybe she hadn't fallen at all, but had just given up her escape bid because of the dark and fallen asleep here. Please let it be that. Please.

He knelt beside her, lifted her head gently. Her cheek on his hand was cold. She didn't stir. He couldn't tell if she was breathing. He felt his own breath coming too fast and too shallow. It was suddenly getting darker. He didn't want her to die. Not to die. He'd never meant for her to die.

He knelt still for a long time, cradling her head on his lap as he grew very slowly calmer. Some of her hair hung down over his knees, and he stroked it over and over, ever so lightly brushing away the cobwebs and the cereal-smelling dust. There was a lot of that dust stuck to her face, especially around her nose and mouth. He thought, even in the half-light, that he could just see it moving slightly. She was breathing! She was breathing! He realised for the first time that he knew her name now, and for the first time he called her by it, speaking to her in a low, kind, coaxing voice. He was coaxing her to live. To live. He thought she opened her eyes and looked up at him. He thought he saw just the faintest hint of a smile when he called her by her name. He thought so.

And then eventually he became aware of how much his legs ached from kneeling in the same position and he had to move, laying her aside very gently, tenderly ensuring that her face this time was up out of the dust and dirt. And now he was almost certain that she was breathing, because he thought there was a slight sob as he lay her head back on the floor.

He thought his head was going to explode. He didn't know what to do next. He must clear his head. He must get himself calm so he could think. He reached into his jacket pocket for the cigarettes and matches.

*

It was a difficult decision for the editor of the evening paper. The missing little girl was still the story on everyone's lips. But the warehouse fire was new. And they had some great pictures. The chief fire officer said it would be like a bomb going off with all that dry malt dust. And then of course all those old timbers, tinder-dry at heart and covered with creosote. It might have been designed to make a good blaze. They would probably never know what started it, but one spark might be all it took to set the thing going like a furnace. Thank heavens no one was hurt. Well, almost certainly not. It was highly unlikely anyone was inside – though if they had been, no one would ever know, would they?

The Temple at Zelalie

Clive

The sign said, "NO ADMITTANCE EXCEPT FOR AUTHORIZED PERSONNEL", so I barged straight in. Well, I tried to, but the door was locked, and it took me a couple of minutes work with a jemmy to get in. I tried to work as quietly as I could, but you can't jemmy open a stout door quietly, and by the time I got in I was sure the guards were on their way.

Once inside, I looked around for somewhere I could hide in such a way that I could surprise them. I thought there'd probably only be two of them. I certainly hoped so. I'd worked myself up into a frenzy to be brave enough to come here at all, but I was beginning to feel a bit shaky.

It turned out there was only one of them, and he wasn't the brightest guard ever. He didn't even look in the obvious hiding place behind the door as he came in, and I had his throat in the crook of my elbow before he'd even seen me.

"Don't make a sound or try anything funny, and I'll let you breathe. One false move and I'll stop you breathing again."

"Okay. Thanks. Who the devil are you and what are you doing here?"

Well, that's not my idea of not making a sound, but he was talking very quietly and I didn't think anyone who'd not already heard me jemmying the door would have heard him.

He didn't talk much like a guard – at least, not the
way I'd imagined a guard would talk. He didn't seem
to think like a guard, either – at least, not the way I'd
imagined a guard would think.

"I'm Maria. I've come from the village. If I'm not
back in the village in a couple of hours, unhurt, they're
going to tear this place down, stone by stone. They
don't want to do that, they know a lot of people will
get hurt and some might get killed, but they can do it if
they have to. You know that. Do you understand?"

"Yes, I understand. Nobody's going to hurt you, and
you'll be back in your village soon enough. Now can I
have my neck back?"

"Okay."

I let him go. I'd played my only card. Either it would
work or it wouldn't.

"Does anyone else know you're investigating a
break-in?"

"No, but it doesn't matter. Your village friends
couldn't tear this place down if they tried, but no-one's
going to hurt you anyway, and you'll get home in
plenty of time. Why did you come here? What do you
want?"

"I've been sent to ask some questions."

"Go on then. Ask away."

"We want to know what this place is for. Why is it
near our village? Why is it so different from the
temples near the other villages? Why do we have to
keep providing food for all of you, when none of you
do any work at all? Why don't some of you come and
help on the land?"

"You've been feeding us all your lives, and your
parents and grandparents and great-grandparents did

before you – and you don't know why? We do do work here, very important work."

"I still don't see why we should have to feed you. You don't do anything for us."

"Your ancestors have always fed us. They accepted that it was the way it had to be."

"Our parents still say we should feed you. But this is our time now, and we've agreed that we must at least question why."

"Fair enough. But you'll have to be ready to learn some very complicated stuff."

"I can do that. I've got one of the sharpest minds in the village – that's why I was trusted to be the one to come here."

And because I'm a tough nut who doesn't take no for an answer, and because I'm a girl who can out-fight most of the men, I thought, but I didn't mention that.

"It's not something anyone could learn in a couple of hours. You'll have to come again another day, and again, and again. If you're really sharp you'll maybe learn enough to understand what we do here in a couple of years."

"I've got to have something to tell them back in the village today, though."

"And I'll have some explaining to do to the rest of the people here, if you're going to be coming here again and again. The main thing you can tell your villagers is that we're friendly, not people to hate and fear. And that you'll be coming here regularly for science lessons."

I wondered what on Earth science lessons were, and why, if the gods were friendly, none of them had ever spoken to any of us before. But there were specific questions I needed answers to to take back.

"I've still got to explain to the village council why we have to keep feeding you. It's all very well to say you have important work to do and that you'll explain it to me eventually, but it's not important to the people in the village. They're fed up of feeding extra mouths."

"Believe me, it's very important to you, as much as it is to us."

"I don't see how."

"Without us doing what we do, everyone around here would get sick and die. At first it wouldn't be very bad. But after a while it would get very bad, and we – villagers as much as scientists – would all die out in just a generation or two."

That sounded very like what the gods had said in Obridan, but the villagers pulled down the temple there anyway, and nothing bad happened afterwards at all. Inside the temple, they found two very scared young guards, eight of the girls who'd gone missing from Obridan over the years, and the gods – who were just three very fat old men.

The 'just a generation or two' touch was clever, though. It was only a couple of years since they'd pulled down the temple in Obridan, but the gods there had promised instant retribution, and it hadn't happened. You could die worrying about something that wasn't supposed to happen for years.

But this temple was different. You could see the stones Obridan temple was made of. As far as anyone could see, this temple was all carved out of one piece of stone, and not some soft, easily carved stone, either.

This god probably wasn't lying when he said we couldn't tear his place down if we tried. And he'd promised to explain to me what it was they were doing to keep us safe, and what the hazard that they were keeping us safe from was. Even if it was going to take a year or two to explain.

"Your temple is different from the temples in other places. Why aren't there temples like this one near any other villages?"

"Actually, there are labs very like this one in other places – but they're a very long way away, that's why you've never heard of them."

I felt I'd got enough to keep everyone happy for a while, given that I was going to be coming back to learn more, but there was plenty of time before people back in the village would start worrying about me. I'd begun to quite enjoy my chat with the god – he really seemed quite a decent sort, not a bit like the Obridan gods. Not that I'd ever seen the Obridan gods, but I'd heard what people said about them.

"You're not really a guard at all, are you? You're one of the gods, aren't you!"

"No, I'm not a god or a guard, and this isn't a temple. There are no guards, and no gods, here. But I think you'll have to have quite a few lessons before you can really understand what this place is, or who I am."

Thus began my regular attendances at the temple – I mean the laboratory. I still had to do my share of the work in the village, I didn't want to risk being accused of joining the gods in their parasitic existence. I didn't know how long the rest of the young adults in the village would accept my assurances without more detailed explanation, but if it was going to take me a year to learn enough to understand, how quickly would I be able to explain it to them? I didn't feel very confident.

I got to know the gods – scientists – very well, and came to understand why they didn't mix at all with the villagers. I felt very privileged to be allowed into their temple – I'd actually become one of the authorized personnel! There were seventeen of them, most of them my parents' age or thereabouts. Grimm, the god whom I'd first met, was the only one as young as me.

Grimm was a trainee, and he was the only one who regularly had enough free time to spend teaching me. We spent an hour and a half together every day. The first few days, he showed me all around the laboratory – that was a new word to me, and I'd no idea what it meant – and introduced me to everyone. I felt very uncomfortable meeting them, because they seemed very uncomfortable meeting me. They didn't shake my offered hand, and they seemed to try to avoid breathing in my presence. I felt as though they thought I was dirty – and later I learnt that that was exactly how they felt.

Grimm was different. He accepted me as I was, completely. He explained to me about hygiene and cleanliness – and how he understood perfectly that village hygiene was actually pretty good in a practical sense if not a cosmetic one, and that laboratory hygiene was often more apparent than actual. "And that's even in a laboratory like this, dedicated to keeping the environment clean."

I didn't understand what he meant by that. Even in the village we understood very well how dirty the environment was. Or we thought we did.

I learnt a great deal in the first few months, and Grimm was very pleased with me. But I felt as though I wasn't really learning what I wanted to know. None of what I was learning seemed to explain what all this interesting science was for, why it was so important to everyone, not just to the scientists. I was finding it increasingly difficult to persuade my peers in the village that I wasn't just fobbing them off, too.

Then one day when I arrived at the lab, I was met by Petra, the chief scientist, instead of Grimm. Petra was wearing a mask and gloves, even though she knew I always scrubbed myself very clean before coming. "Grimm's very ill," she said, "he won't be able to see you for a while. Please don't come for the next couple of weeks. After that, we'll see if he's fit enough to see you."

That made my life very difficult. I was sure Grimm really was very ill, and I hoped he would be all right, but my peers were sceptical. "Don't you see, they're just fobbing you off now. You wait, in two weeks' time they'll tell you he's still too ill to see you. Or they just won't open the door for you at all."

Luckily Rita backed me up. "We can wait two weeks. We'll see what really happens in two weeks' time."

I felt very nervous climbing the hill to the laboratory on the fourteenth day. The laboratory looked as forbidding as it had that first day, when I'd broken in –

and this time I didn't have the adrenalin I'd worked up in the meeting when I'd been chosen to do the deed. I hoped against hope that Grimm would open the door to me.

But it was a stranger who opened the door. "You must be Maria," she said, "I've been looking forward to meeting you." And she offered me her hand – ungloved.

"How's Grimm?"

I had to know.

"I'm sorry. I think you'd become quite attached to Grimm, hadn't you? Come in, sit down."

I knew then how Grimm was. "No! He's not dead, is he?" My guts knotted up inside me and I felt physically sick.

"He died two days ago. I'm sorry."

I couldn't say anything for a while, and the stranger didn't say anything either, but she put her hand on my forearm and held it gently.

"He caught some village disease from me, didn't he! We've all got immunity to the ordinary village diseases, but he hadn't."

"No, it wasn't a village disease. We're immunized against all the village diseases. It was a leak down in the repository, a bigger one than anyone was ready for. They've contained it now, but Gretel and Fiana also got a big dose, and they are very ill as well. I don't know if we'll save them, but it's looking more hopeful by the day. Some of the others are ill too, but not in danger."

"Who are you, anyway?"

"My name's Margret. I've transferred here from Imienda – but of course you've no idea where Imienda is."

Actually, I did have some idea where Imienda was – Grimm's lessons weren't confined to science, he'd been teaching me geography, too, amongst other things. But I'd no idea how anyone could possibly have come all the way from Imienda in just a few days, or how the people in Imienda had known about the leak so quickly.

"Just now, things are pretty hectic here, with so many ill, me being new on this site, and another temp who doesn't know the place either. We've got no-one spare to give you lessons for a few days. But if you come up here again in three or four days' time, I'll try and pick up where Grimm left off."

Margret was very good, but she wasn't Grimm. I missed Grimm.

Margret wanted to teach me. Grimm had helped me to learn. I could ask Grimm questions about anything, and he'd do his best to answer them. Margret planned what she wanted to teach me, and stuck to her plan.

It wasn't only his superior teaching skills I missed though. I missed Grimm himself. A lot.

I wanted to know how Margret and Bryn had come all the way from Imienda so quickly, and how they'd known so quickly that they were needed, but I couldn't even get through to her that I knew where Imienda was, and how far it was. But over the next few months I did learn a lot about geology, chemistry, energy and especially radioactivity, which was what she knew I needed to understand to explain to the village council why the laboratory was so important.

Finally, the village council met in the village square one evening almost a year after the meeting where I was delegated to break into the laboratory.

"This isn't going to be easy to explain. It's taken me a long time to learn enough to understand what the laboratory do, and why it's so important to us as well as to the scientists who work there."

The questions started straight away. "What's laboratory? What's scientists?"

"Sorry. The laboratory is what we've always called the temple, and the gods are really ordinary people, but they're scientists. It's taken me a long time to learn enough to understand what the scientists in the laboratory do, and why it's so important to us as well as to the scientists who work there."

"Partly that's a matter of trust. Hopefully you'll trust me in a way that you wouldn't have trusted one of them if they'd come down here a year ago and tried to say this in as few words as I'll have to use. Hopefully you'll trust me in a way that I didn't trust them when they explained things to me at first."

"Partly it's a matter of language. They talk the same language we do – more or less. But a lot of the words they use without thinking about them were quite unfamiliar to me a year ago, like scientist and laboratory. I'm afraid I might use them without thinking now, I've got so familiar with them. Stop me if I use words you don't understand."

For a while, someone or other was stopping me every few moments, but gradually I got used to avoiding words village people wouldn't understand, and gradually they got used to the kind of things I was telling them, and the questions stopped. I was losing my voice by the time I finished, over an hour later.

Well, I thought that was why the questions had stopped, but I was wrong. Most people had simply given up trying to follow.

But Rita had been making valiant efforts. "So what you're saying, Maria, is that long, long ago, there were a lot more people than there are now, and some – quite a lot – of them were very greedy, and wanted to eat far too much, and go everywhere much too fast, and keep themselves warm without having to wear many clothes, and do all kinds of pointless, wasteful things. And they made a lot of rubbish in the process, and one particular kind of rubbish that they made is terribly, terribly dangerous, and they just kept on making more and more and more of it without knowing what they could possibly do with it. I think you called it radioactive waste, is that right? Anyway, now we've got to live in a world with an incredible amount of that dangerous rubbish, and the job of the gods in the temple is to keep it from leaking out and killing us all. Have I got that right?"

"That's pretty much it, yes, Rita. Except that a fair amount of it *has* leaked out, and the health of everyone everywhere is affected by it to some extent. A lot of places are so bad no-one can live there at all any more. But most of it is still well contained, and the scientists are trying to minimize the leaks, rather than stop them altogether, which would be impossible."

Ricardo wasn't convinced. "Well, it's a better story than the story the gods in Obridan had, I'll give you that, but it's basically the same story."

Rita came to my rescue again.

"The big, big difference, Mr Ricardo, is that it's our Maria who's told you the story, not some fat, lazy, lying Obridan god."

"They've bought 'our' Maria, that's all that means."

Now it was my turn to get angry.

"No-one's bought me. Yes, I regard those scientists as my friends now. I know how damn hard they work for us all. I can't say I understand everything they do exactly, but I understand enough to know how important it is, and how hard they work. I'm sorry I can't explain it all to you in an hour. Yes, they're my friends. Two of my friends died working to keep you and me safe, Mr Ricardo, and another one nearly died. See my belly? My baby's due any time now. My baby's father died working to keep you and me safe, Mr Ricardo, and you'd better remember that."

I still miss Grimm a great deal. But Rita's always there for me, helping me to raise little Grimm. He's a great kid, with a sharp mind like his dad had, and gentle like him too. Everyone in the village loves him. He's even melted Ricardo's heart.

What kind of world will little Grimm inherit? That's anyone's guess, now that Imienda's been ransacked. We've still got a team of scientists here in Zelalie, but with no training school in Imienda and the big workshops there gone, it's only a matter of time.

I asked Margret about setting up a training school here, but she says that for one thing there's too big a gap between what we learn in the school in the village and what scientists need to be able to do, and for another they don't have the equipment a training school needs. She says that long ago there used to be several training schools in different places around the world, but that Imienda was the last one.

Bunker II

Stephen

So we now return to Colin. Let's take a moment to examine him as he sleeps. He is currently dressed in a shabby England shirt that has seen better days, a pair of fake combats that are ingrained with the dirt of cleaning and amateur horticulture and over all of this he has an expensive yet cheap looking Japanese robe. His hair is that of a lazy alternative in that it has been dyed and styled numerous times but has since been left to run wild. He is currently trapped by the beard fad but strands of gingery blond hair do not cut it in the bars he frequents.

Colin is twenty-nine and aware that he has seen his best years. If it weren't for his crop and his amazing digs he would have very little going for him. He realized some time ago that he could in fact just live in the Bunker and never leave. It really is enormous and stocked up to enable a thousand people to survive a minimum of twenty years. According to the coffee stained manual that lies on a table beside him.

Colin is something of a techie. But the ancient machines that run the Bunker may as well have been built by aliens. They look cool, very sixties sci-fi but the concept of plug-n-play, or even point and click, had not been created when they had been set up. He has however managed to rig his Playstation to the huge CRT monitor in the main control room.

Back in the main entrance we have an argument.
Well, that's a polite word for what they are doing, a
less polite word would be bickering.

We've examined Colin so it's only fair we take a
look at these three. We'll start with Howard. Howard is
in his late middle age. Currently he is still wearing his
security uniform which, despite his time in the army, is
also extremely shabby. He had at first taken care of it
but when it became clear that no one cared and he
wasn't going to get an allowance to maintain it, he
stopped. He's proud of his time in the army, and rightly
so, but its fair to say that a store house in Aldershot
isn't the most dangerous posting in the world. He's
been divorced for some time but still wears the ring for
sentimental reasons. Those reasons don't stretch to him
keeping it on when he goes out drinking and certainly
not when he turns up in Berrenton's lone strip club.

Desmond. Desmond is of course in a suit and tie. It's
a decent old one from Marks and Sparks and his wife is
able to maintain it in a respectable condition. She can
do nothing about his shirts however and after the mad
dash it is now drenched in sweat. His thin blond hair is
plastered to his skull mercifully covering quite how
thin it has become. Although in the right light it looks
like he's already bald. It is perhaps unfair to be too
cruel to Desmond. He is after all a man out of time. He
would have been perfectly at home in the planning
office that designed the bunker with its casual sexism
and guilt-free nicotine. But it is fair to say that
Desmond's best days are behind him too. He just didn't
know it. Desmond peaked back in the halcyon days of
uni, battling in the student union elections and drinking
in the rugby club. (He got a third by the way.)

And then we have Mary. Mary is perhaps the smartest of the group and certainly the youngest. Mary carries a slight amount of extra weight well but was horrified to discover that this impacted on people's perception of her intelligence. And meant that she seldom had eye contact with anyone she was talking to. But once she understood her predicament she dyed her hair blond and learnt how to simper. She too is a university graduate but a rather more successful one. However the main thing she came away from her business finance degree with was a battered copy of The Princess and a plan to retire by forty. She was well on her way too until she made the tactical mistake of hooking up with Desmond. A mistake she now bitterly regrets. She is wearing a flattering and stylish pant suit and is conscious of the fact she isn't wearing any knickers.

DESMOND – Twenty fucking years?

HOWARD – I'm sure its just a suggestion, when things settle down we'll be able to open it again.

DESMOND – Settle down? We don't even know what happened? We don't even know if anything happened at all, it could have been a mouse chewing through a wire.

Mary is checking her mobile phone. Unsurprisingly given that she is in a lead-lined reinforced concrete bunker, she's having trouble getting a signal. Now Mary is smart, but she's flustered so instead of realizing that the chances of getting a signal this deep are slim to say the least, she turns it off and on again.

HOWARD – Look, just calm down. Let's take stock of the situation.

A good suggestion all in all. Howard feels his chest puff out as he considers himself to be rising to the occasion.

Mary drops her phone into a pocket with a huff and glances around the room. It appeared to be a large reception hall with several passages leading off it. The upgrade to the Bunker's tech system hadn't stretched to the cosmetic so wires and cabling are strung from the ceiling and walls. The floor had been laid with a magnificent mural of the towns coat of arms. An attempt to clean it had been made but resulted in merely moving the dust around. Above the reception desk hang two monitors, both with the message 'Stand By' glowing on them.

DESMOND – Take stock. We are stuck behind five foot of steel in a bomb shelter that you locked us into, that about right?

HOWARD – Look, we just need to find the command centre and override the doors. You should be able to manage that shouldn't you?

Desmond pauses for a moment. He takes a deep breath and tries to control his temper. What he thinks is his temper anyway. That's surely why his hand's gently shaking.

DESMOND – Well if the signs are anything to go by it's that way.

He points down the widest of the three corridors. No-one moves. Something in the corner of her eye makes Mary glance back at the monitors. They had both flickered and gone blank.

HOWARD – Ok then, let's go.

Still no movement. They all look down the corridor. Its battleship grey colour scheme suddenly looked dark and foreboding. They look at each other. They look down the corridor again. At precisely that moment a fluorescent bulb gives up and dies.

HOWARD – Well come on then Desmond, off we go.

He gestures with a hand down the corridor. Desmond bites back a retort and squares himself. As he is about to launch himself down the corridor the sound of an explosion echoes through the bunker followed by a brief burst of machine-gun fire. It would be nice to say that our three react in a heroic fashion. You would perhaps expect that the army veteran at least would react in a manner befitting his training. But no. All three stand petrified like rabbits in a headlight. After a moment standing erect they all seem to wake out of a daze and throw themselves behind the reception desk.

HOWARD – What the hell!!

DESMOND – Shh, they'll hear us

MARY – Who'll hear us? This is a damned tomb.

Poor choice of words perhaps. The three huddle together as a rising crescendo of orchestral music starts. They once again look at each other. After a moment Mary raises her head above the desk. On the two monitors a game logo flashes. She watches in awe as a pointer glides across both screens and clicks on 'Continue Campaign.'

The command centre is exactly as you would hope it would be. It has an Enterprise bridge/Cape Canaveral feel to it. Banks of screens and whirring hard drives. In the middle of the room is what was once a magnificent leather chair, very much in the captain's chair style. Evidently the designers had been proto geeks. The chair is now however a touch shabby, a look that is compounded by Colin slouching in it. All the monitors including the main screen are currently showing Colin's avatar as he heroically mows down waves of aliens. He hits pause briefly and takes a deep lungful of a joint followed by a mouthful of coffee.

He returns his attention to his mission. Behind him Desmond, Mary and Howard enter the command centre and stare around the room open mouthed.

COLIN – Eat Grenade!

A massive explosion rings out from every speaker in the bunker followed by manic giggling from Colin.

His giggling stops when the screens all abruptly go blank.

COLIN – Fuck, not again.

He glances round at the perch where his playstation sits hardwired into a command console. Mary stands frowning at him with the power cable dangling loose in her hand. And then Colin's worst nightmare comes true.

DESMOND – Who the hell are you?

HOWARD – That's Colin the cleaner, isn't it!

Colin sinks back into the chair and takes a long, long drag from his joint.

Let's step away from the Command room for a moment and take a closer look at the Bunker. What, you may ask, powers it? Its natural to assume that the power source is nuclear. But you'd be wrong. There is a reason the Town Hall was built where it was. If we travel down through the layers of the bunker, past the storage chambers and recycling units we eventually come to its heart: a hydroelectric power plant. Built to last with only minimal interference and backed up by an entire floor of back up generators and batteries.

These alone should be enough to last a few years and that's rather fortunate.

If we look closer at the power plant we will find that it is currently running way below capacity. It had originally been designed and placed to take advantage of a vast underground reservoir fed by a fast flowing underground river. The reservoir is also tapped to provide water for the bunker, after going through filtration of course. Also rather fortunate as the filters are working overtime

We shall take a look at the lake, giving ourselves as we do the ability to see in pitch black. It's rather lower than it had once been as the power plant periodically releases more to keep itself fed. Tracking along its length we find that the river that feeds it is now little more than a trickle. A trickle of polluted goop at that. We glide along following the route of the river and very shortly come across the problem. Where once the river had run down an ancient cave system, now that cave system is ruptured with multiple fractures and cracks draining away the majority of the water and polluting what little remains. But we mustn't be to hard on the fracking company that did this, after all, how were they to know? It had only been an experiment, they hadn't even found enough oil or gas to cover the expense. They had made more from the insurance when the project was shut down. But they did learn a lot. If not a lesson.

Mary is examining the games console.

MARY – Is it possible do you think, that this caused the sirens to go off?

Faces

Jack

He sees faces.

Not all the time – intermittently. He's been doing it since he was a child. One moment you can be talking to him perfectly normally; the next he'll be in a corner, shrieking and pointing at you. It's been eighteen years, and he still talks to me about it. He never went to school – he didn't get further than the first day before he attacked another child. He was five, and his classmate wasn't badly hurt, so Ruby and I managed to smooth it over. But we couldn't take him back.

I've tried to get Simon to describe the faces before, but he never gets very far. If he describes them, he sees them. The only thing I know about them is that they're always completely white, with wide black eyes. Sometimes they're trying to speak to him, but he can never quite hear what they're saying. He thinks some of them might be smiling, but it's difficult to tell with their dark, wide mouths. I asked him if they were ghosts, but he told me it wasn't that simple. They're something more – but at the same time, something less. I remember asking him to elaborate, but that was as far as he got before we had to get him into his room again. He's ridiculously strong, especially now he's eighteen, but the bars always hold him. We had them installed when he was very young, and it was a worthwhile investment. I think the door to his bedroom is probably more fortified than the front door to the house.

Ruby and I have taken him to see doctors, of course. They didn't understand what was happening. They told me they're hallucinations. Of course they're hallucinations, anyone could have guessed that. But they were never able to tell me more. They've tried to have Simon sectioned, but we stopped them. It took a lot of time, money and several solicitors, but he's staying with us. He always will, and there's nothing in the world that can stop that. I remember Ruby was in tears as we left. I remember holding her before we got into the car. I can still feel her tears on my cheek, her soft black hair obscuring the building that housed the people who wanted to take my son from me.

Erm…honestly, I've never been sure whether Simon's insane. Apart from the faces, he's always seemed sound enough. He was a quick learner, an early walker, an early speaker. He never had any trouble with his lessons, anyway. He's able and articulate. Of course, all that goes out the window once the faces appear and he becomes a gibbering, screaming mess. I suppose I should have seen it coming, really.

Our home life isn't that complicated. We all wake up at 8am. I go to work, and Ruby teaches Simon. She was a university lecturer once, but had to go on a few extra courses in order to get the qualifications to teach him from home. We manage well enough, though. Lessons finish at 5pm, and I come home at about 6pm from work. Ruby and I spend the remainder of our day studying. We get barely enough sleep to function, but it's still (crucially) enough to function. When he sees the faces, we get him into his room and keep him there until he stops screaming. Like I said, sometimes it takes hours, but he always calms down eventually.

Except that one time.

On that Thursday, the day my life was ruined, I came in from work early. 4pm – Frank let me have the afternoon off. I'd closed a major sale, and was generally feeling pretty impressed with myself. As I locked the front door behind me, I could hear the scratching of pen on paper, and rattling in the kitchen. Ruby had set Simon an essay, and was making supper for us. She'd tied her black hair back tightly, to keep it out of the way of the casserole, and she had my old apron on. She somehow managed to make it look like she could take it down a catwalk. The kitchen looked pretty good too – we'd had it re-done recently, with some of the wooden cabinets replaced with marble ones. Overall, with the marble reflecting the late afternoon light, and the beautiful woman stood in the centre of the kitchen, it looked like something out of a television ad, rather than a real life family home.

I wrapped my arms around her waist, and she giggled.

"Hi, Jerry. You're back early."

"We sold the Rock-Ola." I grinned. "It's been sitting in the warehouse for months, and we finally got rid of it."

Ruby turned, flung her arms out wide, and hugged me properly. "That's great! Was Frank pleased?"

"He was. He was beginning to hate it as much as I was. How's Simon getting on?"

She kissed me on the cheek and turned back to the cooking. "He's getting on with things – better than he was yesterday."

"What's he writing on?"

"Lord of the Flies." Unconsciously, she did a little flourish with the ladle. She was pleased with herself, I could tell. It had always been one of Ruby's favourite books. The blonde, innocent boy next door had been named after one of the characters.

"Finished!"

"Have you done your conclusion?" Ruby spoke without looking round.

"Sort of."

"Let's have a look, Simon." I walked back through the hall towards the living room, Ruby following close behind.

His grin shone at me from across the room as I entered it. He was sitting with his back straight, as ever, at his desk in the corner of the living room, facing away from the TV. As I drew closer, I noticed that he was rapidly outgrowing the desk – his legs were uncomfortably packed away under his chair in order to pull it in properly. I'd have to talk to Ruby about replacing it.

"How did you find it?" I asked, as I started to read.

"Not that difficult." He replied. There was no smugness to his voice – I was always proud of that. "I wasn't sure how sorry to feel for Jack in the end."

"Hm. You can tell slightly – you've got to come down on one side of the fence or the other, otherwise you risk sounding a bit vague. Otherwise, it's good." I straightened, and his face lit up. "How long did this take you?"

"Two hours."

"Hm. Bit slow."

His face fell slightly.

"Was James texting you?" I smiled.

"A few times." Simon admitted grudgingly. "He was trying to talk to me about doing a game tonight. He wants to talk about his girlfriend."

I smiled, hopefully not as sadly as I felt. Simon couldn't play with children face to face, but he'd built some strong friendships with boys he'd met online. Playing video games was about the only way he could interact with children his own age. He'd never met James, and didn't even know what the other boy looked like, but he was the closest friend Simon had.

"Well, fair's fair. Now you've done that essay, your time is your own for a bit."

The grin returned.

"Does this mean I get to go outside?"

"I'll take you to the park for a bit after seven, and we can have a kickabout." I smiled. "Shouldn't be too many people around then."

"Thanks Dad!" he stood and hugged me. "Can we go now?"

I looked at Ruby. "Is there time?"

"Not for anything long, but maybe a few quick games. Casserole is going to be –"

He flipped.

There's never any warning. It just happens. I didn't see him change, because I was facing Ruby at the time. All I felt was a very hard shove, and suddenly I was careering towards the mantelpiece. I hit it. Something broke – I wasn't sure whether it was one of our ornaments, or something of me.

He stood over me, in tears.

"What do you want?" he screeched. "Why are you always here? What do you want?"

The face must have answered him, because he scrambled backwards, and retched on the floor. I tried to take advantage of his momentary weakness, and lunged at him.

I always try not to think about how we look to him. An unsmiling, frozen white face, with deep black eyes, leaping forward to wrap bony arms around his legs. Another blocking the doorway, taking slow, cautious steps towards him to grab him and drag him away.

Maybe they say other things to him while they're doing it. I don't know. He still never tells me.

He got stronger since he hit puberty. Strong enough to break free of my grasp, and kick me in the face. My nose broke, and I yelled, spitting and whimpering as blood gushed from it. I wasn't sure if he ever saw that bit. Maybe he saw the face, and not the blood. Or maybe he saw both, but didn't hear my sobs. Maybe he saw it all. The main thing is, he still didn't recognise me, and he knew that I wasn't coming after him for a while. So he turned to deal with the other one. Ruby.

She was ready, blocking the door. Simon simply charged at her, screaming all the while. He barrelled into her, and both of them disappeared in a tangle out in the hall.

He kicked her, and I heard her grunt as all the air went from her lungs. The thundering crash that followed seconds later was, I assume, Simon slamming into the door. Through the pain haze, I could hear the panicked banging as Simon desperately tried to hammer his way out.

As I heard Ruby talk to him, I moaned. I didn't have the energy to scream.

"Simon, you can't get out. Come on. Come with us."

She'd forgotten that he doesn't see us. And if he ever hears us, it won't be us saying it. It'll be them.

It almost never happens, but this time, I think Simon did hear the words.

I think that's what killed him.

Somehow, I managed to get to the door. I could barely see – my vision was blurred from the tears in my eyes, and every tiny movement caused an explosion of pain from the centre of my face. Ruby had managed to get to her feet, though she was dizzy. Simon crashed into her again, punching her. He caught her on the side of her head, but she stayed standing. He hit her a few more times, each strike more fierce than the last. She tried to protect her head, so he attacked her body instead.

I watched my son beat my wife to the floor.

I dithered.

Too many thoughts were trying to force their way through my head at once. I had to pin his arms. I had to protect her. Then there was something else. I had to take him somewhere after that.

He hit her again.

But where?

He hit her again.

I didn't know what to do. If I took another strike to the head, it'd incapacitate me. But I didn't want to hurt either of them, which I definitely would do if I dived in.

Simon hit Ruby yet again, and her eyes rolled, blood trickling from a cut above her eyebrow.

I made a snap decision, and grabbed Simon by the waist, hauling him off Ruby, who didn't move. I spun to face him, but he didn't attack me. Tears were streaking his face, which was completely drained of blood.

"Let me out!" he snapped.

"No." I muttered the word, answering him before I knew what I was doing. I never found out whether he heard me.

"LET ME OUT!" he screamed, and then charged, arms flailing.

His palm caught me just above the eye, temporarily blinding me. The pain from my nose flared, and I vomited into the hall. Simon hadn't stopped, running past me into the kitchen.

I spat, and crawled to Ruby, whose eyes were fluttering. She was murmuring something, but I hushed her. I tried to haul her to her feet, but she lapsed into unconsciousness again. I left her – I couldn't risk leaving Simon alone too long.

He was waiting for me in the kitchen. As soon as I set a foot across the threshold, he spun round, and slashed at me with one of the knives Ruby had been using to cook. I fell, a deep cut on my chest. Until I saw him standing over me with the knife in his hand, it hadn't honestly occurred to me that any of us might die that day. There was smoke in the air, and a strong smell of burning from the abandoned casserole. His face loomed through it, and suddenly the knife was at my throat.

"All the windows are barred. The doors too. Let me out."

I just stared at him, praying he wouldn't decide to use the knife again. He wasn't seeing me.

The face must not have replied either. His face, still wild-eyed, suddenly snarled, and he buried the knife in my leg.

I screamed, and blacked out.

It was two, maybe three minutes before I woke, a rhythmic, hollow thudding echoing through my head. The pain set in almost immediately. I moaned, and clasped my hand round the handle of the knife, but I couldn't pull it out. I simply didn't have the strength.

The thudding continued. I looked up, to my left.

Simon was banging his head against the marble. He was soaked in blood – his own. He'd tried to cut his wrists, but it hadn't worked. His eyes were glazed, and there was no expression on his face. In a sense, he was probably dead before I woke. He'd swing his head back, hold it there for a few seconds, and then throw it forward to get the maximum velocity, connecting with a sickening crack. Over and over and over again.

It took him about five minutes until he fell to the tiles, blood splashing. I couldn't tell which of it was his, and which was mine. He hadn't knocked himself unconscious. I knew. If you were there, you'd say that too. It was just the way he fell.

Simon was dead.

This wasn't all that long ago. Maybe four months? My chest wound wasn't serious, and Simon had concussed me in addition to breaking my nose. He did the real damage to my leg, though – I'm told I won't ever walk without a limp. Hence the wheelchair, at the moment. It's easier than crutches.

Erm, I haven't seen much of Ruby. She's not really in touch with reality anymore. She's in Kent, which is where, I think, she'll stay. She still makes casserole for Simon occasionally, and sits down to teach him. The orderlies let her do it. I visited her once or twice, but she didn't recognise me, so I didn't go back. I prefer to remember her like she was, before she lost all that weight. And most of her hair. And her mind.

She never mentions the faces to them. Ruby's imaginary world is actually preferable to her real one – she remembers the highlights of Simon. She's removed any hint of the faces from her little universe. Sometimes I wish I could live there.

I'm fine, thanks. I'm spending a bit of time at my friend Ryan's house. I can't go back to my own. He's been really good to me – he hardly ever lets me out of his sight. I spend a lot of time reading – it's my way of escaping. I've not killed anyone, if that's what you're asking me. I told everyone from the beginning that I didn't kill Simon. It was a suicide.

You know, I don't think you do believe me. I'm a bit sick of this, being treated like I'm a criminal, or as if I'm insane. I'm not dangerous. I'm trying to spend my days trying to forget about it, or at least trying to ignore it, and you people drag me down here to this tiny little room, with your neutral expressions, and your tape recorders, clasping your hands like that. I've told you what happened, and whatever evidence you've gathered has to support me. He died.

Don't call me Jerry. You don't know me. Don't you dare act as if you know me. Get out – I want to talk to Simon.

Stop calling me Jerry. Simon's not dead, how can he be dead? I'm looking at him, he's there!

Of course it's Simon, I know my son when I see him. Ryan, look, tell them that's Simon.

Doctor? Doctor who? That's my friend Ryan; I'm staying at his house. I don't think he's a doctor, not unless they're accepting business graduates now. Look, can we have this discussion after I've talked to Simon, he's just finished his essay, and he wants me to look it over. We always do it.

Simon, don't listen to them. Get on with your maths for now, maybe Mum will be with you in a minute. Now listen, Ryan, I – Ryan? Why is your face like that? Who are you? Let go – take your hands off me. Where's Ryan? I said, let go. LET GO. LET GO OF ME NOW. WHO ARE YOU?

WHERE'S RYAN? WHERE AM I? SIMON! SIMON I DON'T

The Prisoner

Clive

A man is in a prison cell. It's a very comfortable prison – it's warm and dry, he's well fed, and he has plenty of books, writing paper, and writing implements. The furniture is comfortable, and he has a nice writing desk. The guards disturb him once every twenty minutes all day, so he can't concentrate on his reading or writing as he'd like, but even so – a comfortable prison.

His cell has one window. Outside is a dingy street, grey and dirty. It's often deserted apart from rats and mangy dogs running everywhere. When there is anyone there, they're filthy, dressed in rags, shouting at each other and fighting. The weather is foul every day – raining and cold, with a biting wind driving the rain into everyone's rags. It seems to have been like that for years.

Then one morning they move him to a different cell, looking out onto fields, trees, a pretty river, and a lovely waterfall. The same day, the weather brightens dramatically – it's sunny and warm. There are children laughing and playing in the fields, and lambs skipping about. The wind is just a gentle breeze – just enough to make the leaves of the trees rustle, which he can hear in the gaps in the children's laughter.

Conditions inside his cell are same as they were in the other cell.

His desire to escape from his prison was very weak before – imagine how it's changed!

The next morning he wakes up, and finds the second cell was a dream anyway. Does he still want to escape from his prison? Or does he want to escape back into the dream?

Or is he dreaming now, and was the second cell reality?

Finally Free

Marko

The world was a giant surface of white and I stood in the middle of it, surrounded by nothing but wind and snow. Suddenly the imaginary path I was following turned red. I stopped and looked back for a second. The setting sun broke free near the horizon and painted everything red.

Snow and fire.

On the ground behind me, the footsteps I made just a minute ago started disappearing under the freshly fallen snow. It felt right, somehow.

The snow glittered, energized by strong winds and the last rays of sunlight of the day. It was a strange, calming sight; accompanied by thoughts of absolution and achievement. I have been waiting for this all my life, I realize that now.

Life entwined me with its own realities, plans and schemes, but this is what I was always meant to do. I guess I needed to grow older, collect all those little victories and defeats Life brings; experiences and memories; failures and lessons, before I was ready to make such a radical step.

Of course now, standing here, looking at the summit I was visiting in my dreams so many times, the decision to abandon everything and come here doesn't seem that radical or extreme. It feels... natural, as if

Life led me here; as if I would have ended up here anyway in the end.

I smiled, remembering how scared I was, so many times.

Our lives feel so real, of course I was scared. All that struggle, to succeed, to excel, to build a career, to earn more money, to prove yourself worthy in society's eyes… it all feels so real, so right, so meaningful. Until you realize it's not. Until you gather the courage to step out if it, follow the comforting sounds in your heart. It is just one step, frightening and seemingly impossible, but once you make it; you never want to go back.

I have waited for 55 years and almost lost my chance. First, I was too young, I wanted my place in the world; too deaf to listen to what my heart was really saying and too eager to prove what I was capable of, to myself and others. Then there was a wife, a house, children, career. Most of it was beautiful, rich and fulfilling. There were moments of such power and so much love I thought my heart would burst. There were moments of such despair I saw no light and no reason to live.

That, I know it now, is the biggest power of Life – it all feels so real it is next to impossible to get out of its shackles. It is real, until you are ready to listen to the voice in your heart telling you there is more in to it than you think; much more than what everyone else around you is telling you; much more than most of the people ever think.

I was 55 when that voice became louder than the noise of what I though Life was. My wife died in a car accident a year before; my children all grown up, busy with their own illusions; drowning their dreams in shallow lakes of everyday.

I was sitting in my kitchen, surrounded by stuff I had been gathering and fighting for all my life. It was snowing outside and I could feel the streets being covered by those soft, fluffy white flakes of frozen rain. A hot cup of tea in front of me kept my fingers warm. It was just a normal day, I realized. Just like all these yesterdays, people outside were waking up, having their breakfasts and going to work. Some women stayed home with the kids, some went out to shop, and some worked. Some men worked, some got fired, some just lay in their beds. Kids were playing, crying, running and jumping. The world's heartbeat went on as it always did.

As I watched the snowflakes melting on my window, and wondered where they were yesterday, the scale of it all hit me. It was just a thought, but I realized we are reducing life to such a small, insignificant scale, and make so much fuss over it. Every single day.

For the first time ever, I allowed myself to be overwhelmed by everything around me. I tried to sense the scale of this world, to feel everything that was happening this very instant only on this planet. That very thought set me free.

I made no calls, I sent no letters, wrote no emails. I sold the house; burnt all the bridges. I said my goodbyes silently and just left. I had an image in my head, of a snow-covered mountain top that barely ever felt the touch of a human foot. I had the image of a freedom I denied myself for lifetimes and now, for the first time ever, I'm ready to stare at its face.

My journey has finally begun.

Bunker III

Stephen

It is of course *not* the games console that caused the alarm to trip. Our heroes will work this out but only after much argument. We however can safely know the truth. An apocalypse has in fact occurred but the future of humanity does not rely on these four. Quite what happened may remain a mystery for the moment but suffice to say that billions have died in pain and agony and the suffering has been quite horrific.

Back in the Command Room however.

COLIN – What alarm?

HOWARD – What alarm! How the hell long have you been down here?

Howard, despite his job, is not the most perceptive of people. Mary on the other hand is looking at a pile of pizza boxes that lie heaped next to the command chair.

MARY – Long enough, I should say. Months, at a guess.

COLIN – Well nobody else was using it.

DESMOND – A squatter? On council property!

COLIN – What alarm?

Howard strides towards Colin with the intent to put him in an arm lock.

HOWARD – The alarm that locked us in here, you little prick!

He makes a grab for Colin who slips away and places the command chair between them. He ducks down slightly and peers over the chairs back.

DESMOND – Let's not start that, you've been here for longer than us, is there an override for the doors?

COLIN – Override?

HOWARD – Come here you little shit!

He makes another grab for Colin who swings the chair round to maintain its position between them. Howard finds himself instead lunging into the pizza box pile and scattering boxes and old pizza crusts across the floor.

DESMOND – Really this isn't helping. How about an outside phone line?

He looks around and notices one of many phones that line the Command room. He picks one up and places it to his ear.

DESMOND – Hello?

Not knowing what else to do he does what he's seen in many films and jiggles the lever in the cradle a few times.

DESMOND – Hello?

Still nothing.

Behind him Howard makes another lunge for Colin but this time comes into contact with a large rotating ashtray which goes flying across the room, covering him in a cloud of ash.

DESMOND – Look gentlemen, this really isn't helping.

HOWARD – This little shit got us locked in here, And he's trespassing on council property. I'm gonna bounce him off the walls.

He lunges again and despite how stoned he is Colin once again rotates the chair, skips over some empty boxes and picks up his joint before it starts a fire. He looks at it for a second and then takes a drag.

HOWARD – Is that drugs?

Colin exhales at him.

COLIN – You tell me.

He then ducks his head behind the back of the chair again.

Every monitor in the room flickers for a moment but neither Howard or Colin is paying any attention and Desmond is trying more phones.

Howard issues a low growl and tries again to grab Colin but he steps on a pizza box and slips landing heavily on his back. Colin peers over the chair at him and lets out a brief bark of laughter and then ducks back down.

MARY – Gotcha.

She has finished removing Colin's botch job and has managed to reset the command console he had cannibalized to play games. The lights in the Command room go out.

We have already seen too many expletives so we will ignore what the three gentlemen all shout out.

After a moment the system reboots. Each individual monitor returns to its previous purpose. The main screen now displays the clock countdown. The speaker system emits a squeal of feedback.

BUNKER – All occupants to designated works stations. Security Protocols are in effect.

COLIN – Well that doesn't sound ominous.

BUNKER – All occupants to designated work stations. Stand by for orders from RECC Senior Officer. Security Protocols are in effect.

Desmond stands erect and tugs at his suit. He attempts to shot his cuffs in the Bond style but fails and quickly stops trying.

DESMOND – Well that would be me, where is the Senior Officer's station?

He quite naturally starts walking towards the command chair. Howard has by now returned to his feet and is ineffectually trying to brush the ash and bits of tomato sauce from his uniform.

HOWARD – Who says that's you? I'm the senior security officer here.

DESMOND – With the greatest respect Howard, I'm the senior elected official here.

HOWARD – bollocks, you're a flunky. I'm the senior officer here. I'm the *only* officer here.

The two of them are now squaring off. This does not look as impressive or intimidating as they both hope it does.

MARY – Look, it doesn't matter. We still don't know what's going on, we need an outside line.

COLIN – Ha!

Mary rounds on him.

MARY – This is a cold war era bunker, it will have an internet connection.

COLIN – Bollocks.

MARY – What do you think it was created for in the first place? Arpanet, it's the spine that the internet was built on and this place will have a connection to it or it serves no fucking purpose at all. 'Regional control' you dickhead.

Colin and Mary are now squaring off. This doesn't look any more impressive. Especially given Colin can't stop himself from glancing at Mary's chest. He is stoned, let's not think too harshly of him.

The four of them face off, at an impasse for the moment. As such they are all once more shocked when the lights shut down once more to be replaced by red emergency lights.

BUNKER – Warning, Warning. RECC Senior Officer to command centre.

Desmond looks around slightly bewildered.

DESMOND – But Im here?

COLIN – This is not good.

The red lights cut out once more and the regular lighting returns. On the main monitor the countdown has vanished and is replaced with a Playstation boot screen.

MARY – Well ok, that should give us some breathing space. How long have you been down here Colin?

COLIN – A few months.

MARY – And the system hasn't done anything like this before?

COLIN – Nope.

MARY – Ok... Have you found anything that may help us make sense of this?

This is a stretch and she knows it. But fortunately Colin has a positive answer.

COLIN – Well, there's the manual.

The Bunker is, as I may have mentioned, vast. Colin has barely scratched the surface in his frequent explorations. He has been considerably more careful since he once got lost for a day. This problem was caused in a very traditionally British manner. When the planning had been done it had included a system of maps and guides to help people navigate around it.

This system had then been farmed out for a small sub company to handle. While this company had been busy the building work itself had changed significantly so when the guide system was ready it was already hopelessly out of date.

Rather than install it it had been decided to restart the project and really get it right. And it had in fact been completed. The finished system, or at least the plans for them, had been sent to the MOD department that handled the Bunker on the 10th of November 1989. A day after the fall of the Berlin Wall.

The Jennyheg Stones

John

Roughly 5 miles to the east of the Westmorland village of Heymanceaux is the remains of an abandoned village. Known to the locals as Wattanby, the village appears in local records (including the Domesday book – *Waettenelburgha*) up until the time of the black death; when it appears to have been abandoned.

Local legend tells things differently.

Just to the north of the ruins is a small henge-like structure that is known as the Jennyheg stones. Stories name it as the home of a notorious witch: Jenny the Hag. She was – it is said – notorious for being cantankerous, and casting hexes upon neighbours' farm animals. Eventually the villagers had had enough and called upon their Liege Lord for assistance; who sent his eldest son to deal with the problem.

A confrontation occurred, and Jenny was said to have thrice cursed those who confronted her: their weapons would be "as brittle as bark," their heirs would "falter and fall without honour" and their lands would be "barren and burnt as the sun." The lord's son – hearing enough – drew his sword and drove through her body. She died, but as he pulled out the weapon it caught in her ribs, and snapped off. The villagers buried her where she fell, as the local priest refused to allow her to be buried in hallowed ground. Yet her curse was said to come true, and the village of

Wattanby was burnt to the ground as a result of a lightning strike that very night.

A nineteenth century clergyman and local historian, Thomas Halliday, suggests that this story is an explanation for the unusual effigy in the nearby 12th century church of St Michael. This is of Sir Stephen de Galwen; and shows him lying in state in armour (as was the style) but his sword is two thirds of the length of weapons at the time, and is missing its end. Stephen died during the hundred years war, not in battle, but of dysentery whilst on campaign in Northern France.

However, an archeological dig at the Jennyheg stones in the 1960s revealed a grave at the edge of the site. On investigation, the body within was shown to have a piece of rusted metal about a hand's breadth long lodged within its spine at about the location of the heart.

A similar dig ten years later at Wattanby revealed a layer of scorched earth around almost all the structures, and analysis of some of the remaining stones showed non-visible evidence of intense heat.

Modern dating techniques applied to both the remains at the stones and the village puts the timing of both of these to within roughly five years of each other; and the period in question also encompasses the noted date of the death of Stephen de Galwen.

It is interesting to note that the de Galwen family up to that point had been steadfast vassals of of Earl of Westmorland, with evidence for them fighting for the Earl since the Conquest. However the family name disappears from the County Rolls in the 14th century, and nothing is heard of the family after that.

Not Like Most Girls

Jack

"I'm not having this conversation every time. It's absolutely out of the question."

"Why? It's been almost two years."

Cara turned to him. "David. You categorically cannot meet my parents."

"Do they have something against solicitors?" She shook her head. "It's nothing to do with that."

David scowled. "What then? Puritans?"

Cara unbuckled her seatbelt and fought the urge to smile. "Not exactly. Look, just trust me on it."

"Is there something you're not telling me?"

The half-smile vanished like a fox down a hole. "What?"

"Not many women in their thirties still live with their parents, Cara. Look, if the situation's delicate, just tell me. I don't need to know details. But only dysfunctional couples keep secrets."

She stared at him, suddenly furious. "You don't know what you're talking about."

"No, I don't." He said coldly.

Cara got out of the car, her heels sinking into the snow.

"That's the damn problem!" He shouted after her.

"You're not meeting my parents, David!" She screamed, stamping her foot. A pair of passers-by let their gazes hit the floor, markedly increasing their pace. "They'll eat you alive!"

"Whatever." David waved a hand dismissively as she slammed the door, and the car peeled away from the pavement.

"Doesn't know what he's talking about." Cara repeated to herself, storming towards the house. Her long black dress swept across the drive, contrasting starkly with the driven snow. As she reached the door, she unconsciously pushed her glasses up her shapely nose – a teenager's habit she'd never been able to suppress.

As she fished her keys from her coat, she fancied she heard movement from inside. But that was impossible – nothing would be moving at this time of night. Beyond the frosted glass, there was nothing but darkness. She put the key in the door, turning it carefully.

Cara stepped into the gloom, her heel just barely catching on the doorstep. She swore quietly, closing the door with a gentle snap.

"Mum?" She half-whispered.

Nothing.

Satisfied, she fumbled for the hall light, turning her back for a split second as a skittering noise echoed down the hallway. She started and spun back, her eyes attempting to pierce the blackness.

"Dad?"

A figure was standing at the end of the hall, framed by the feeble light leaking in from the kitchen beyond. Cara felt her heart pulse in her chest, and her fingers clumsily slapped the wall behind her, searching for the switch.

"Dad?"

Click.

Light flooded the hall, and the figure was gone. Cara leaned against the wall for a second, waiting for her pulse to return to normal. She knew she needed to sleep. She was probably a bit drunk – she'd known that as she'd had her third glass with David earlier. After a few moments, she straightened up, striding down the hall. Some water would do the trick. Maybe a sandwich. Then bed.

She reached the kitchen, and stopped dead. It had been utterly destroyed. Pots and pans were strewn across the room, and the plates had been pulled from the cupboards, their smashed remains scattered across the counters. The cutlery drawers had been launched across the room, and pulverised into splinters. Only an iron chair sat untouched at the table, thick tape hanging from the arms in ribbons. Amongst it all, a pool of red was spreading slowly over the floor, slipping over the smooth tiles.

Cara stared.

"...Mum?"

She said the word softly, as if scared to break the silence.

"MUUUM!"

As if in answer, an inhuman shriek echoed from behind her.

The figure sprinted down the hall, long unnatural legs eating up the distance faster than Cara could process the sight of what was happening.

It slammed into her, still shrieking. Her heels collapsed instantly underneath her and before she knew it she was on the floor, the cutlery and broken plates digging sharply into her back. The pain caused her to arch her body sharply, instinctively throwing her attacker off. It slipped in the pool on the floor, and its head connected with the table with a loud crack. It gibbered, thrashing.

Cara pulled herself painfully up, spotting the bread knife that had she'd missed landing on by bare centimetres. She grabbed it and quickly got to her feet as the creature recovered. It launched itself across the table, turning it over with a crash as it jabbered and spluttered.

She caught it by the throat, thrusting the knife deep into its shoulder. It screamed. An eyeless socket glared at her, and the creature's remaining bulbous eye rolled. Dark splotches of black matted its grey face, which was missing a nose. It gabbled incomprehensibly through broken teeth as its outstretched arms swatted her desperately.

Cara gritted her teeth, driving the knife deeper until she felt bone. The creature let out a single squeal, and then went limp, falling forwards into her expectant arms. She grimly dragged it to the chair, ignoring the pain as she walked across the broken crockery on the floor. Its foot brushed a piece of broken glass, and it whimpered quietly. Cara didn't bother to glance, stopping briefly to scoop up her handbag from where she'd dropped it.

Wrenching the knife from the creature's shoulder, she dumped it unceremoniously into the iron chair. Cara unzipped her handbag, taking a roll of tape from inside. With practised, deliberate movements, she wound it in ever-decreasing circles along the creature's arms, using the bread knife to sever it from the roll.

She straightened up, hands on hips, and surveyed the figure in the chair. Its hands hung limply, and its head rolled on its neck. The tattered remains of its clothes were still attached to parts of its body, and a simple yellow face smiled from the white T-shirt it still partially wore, its broad grin contrasting sharply with the creature's hairless, ugly head.

"Right then." Cara knelt carefully, so she was at eye-level. "Now where's Dad?"

The Meeting

Clive

He was twenty-four. She was only nineteen.

She could type forty words a minute, with perfect spelling and grammar, and a wide and educated vocabulary. He pecked at the keyboard with two fingers, couldn't spell, didn't always hit the key he intended anyway and didn't necessarily notice, and had to look up quite a lot of the words she used.

They'd never met before – not in the flesh, so to speak, anyway. They'd met in an internet chat room over a year earlier, and chatted frequently. They'd seen a couple of still photographs of each other. He'd seen a lot of photographs she'd taken, and she'd seen a few he'd taken, and a few more that other people had taken for him.

They met on a windswept and lonely railway station platform, fifty miles from each of their homes. There was no booking clerk in the ticket office, just an automatic ticket machine. It was doubtful there were any railway staff there at all, but they didn't know for sure one way or the other. She'd travelled from home unaccompanied.

She was well but casually dressed, he was uncomfortable in the unfamiliar shirt and tie and smart trousers. She stood and smiled, looking at him. He looked at the ground, and twisted his fingers together.

He had his little sister – *his little sister* – and his probation officer with him.

Oonagh and Christine. Oonagh was eleven.

Trying to talk was very awkward for both of them. Christine introduced them, as if it was necessary.

Oonagh suggested that it would be okay if she and Christine stayed in the waiting room, out of sight, for up to an hour. Christine said that would be okay, but gave her a panic alarm, and said they could come into the waiting room before the hour was up if they wanted to. She and he both guessed that this was actually all Christine's idea, and that she'd arranged beforehand with Oonagh for her to make the suggestion. They were right.

They didn't hear Christine approaching. She didn't disturb their kiss. She didn't know whether it was their first, but it looked like it.

After a minute, she coughed and they saw her.

"That was an hour?"

" 'Fraid so."

They held hands and pulled away from each other.

"You want to meet again next week?"

"Yes." Both of them, no hesitation.

His Mum didn't approve, and had said so to Christine. Oonagh knew, too, but secretly disagreed. She was quietly excited. Mum would come round. In a way, Mum was relieved that it wasn't her responsibility, that she could leave it to Christine.

*

*

earlier

*

Mum: "What's he doing, meeting some trollop he's found in his computer?"

Oonagh: "Mum, you're a fine one to call her a trollop!"

(Remember, Oonagh is eleven...)

*

earlier still

*

Mum: "The only person who'd ever defend what you did was probably your father."

He: "You always told us you didn't know who our fathers were!"

Mum: "That's right. That's why I called him 'probably your father'..."

The Rain Within

Marko

There was nothing outside but rain. I stood by the window, counting the drops and wondering just how many fall between two heartbeats. Clouds were looming over the city, leaving no trace of the blue sky. I knew it must still be out there, just as the Sun is as well, but at this moment, I felt nothing but the rain; saw nothing but the grey.

The world outside didn't seem to care. An occasional bird would still fly between the park and the roofs, looking for food for its young. Branches moved in silence, touched by the cold, merciless wind. Earth itself lived on as if nothing has happened, and that hurt me more than anything else.

I reached in my pocket and took out a framed photo. You smiled gently at me from it, as you always did when our eyes met. I fought the tears swelling up, leaned my forehead against the cold window, trying not to feel the raindrops on the other side of the glass. I followed a single drop, watched it slide down, drawn by the invisible but ever present force that ultimately gets to us all. The drop didn't mind, though – it will join the river of rain and mud 20 floors below and continue its journey. No one seemed to care, and it was tearing me apart.

There were few people on the street, fighting against the rain and the wind. Some because they had to, others because they wouldn't let the rain dictate their day. The postman struggled with his bag, trying to keep its contents dry as he reached in for someone's mail. An old woman greeted him and complained about the weather. A stray dog glanced at him as he passed by, too wet and cold to care. I shifted my attention from the streets below to the building opposite mine. Some windows were opened, some firmly shut with blinds pulled over them. People lived their lives as they always did when it rained.

Rain muted the sounds, all but its own. Someone was arguing in the flat above mine. A child from downstairs was playing piano, the same simple melody over and over, until it sinks in and she becomes proficient enough playing that part. Then she'll move on to something else. A dog barked somewhere in the building and there was a smell of food being prepared from somewhere on my floor. The rain had a way of changing lives, and no one seemed to notice it but me.

It was everywhere. It crawled between the buildings, it streamed on the streets, and it took over the air. Outside, there was no escaping it. It soaked the clothes, covered faces, dripped from everywhere. People were breathing it in, stepping in it and brushing against it. It was there when you stepped out of the building, waiting for you with undying patience. It was in your eyes as you stepped off the curb. It kept falling as you slipped and fell. It covered the windscreen of the cars passing by. It made you invisible, until it was too late. The rain is evil, I know it now. It changes lives, it stops heartbeats. And no one cares. The postman still delivers his letters, stray dogs still roam. Rain still falls.

Tears streamed down my face and I wiped them dry as roughly as I could. My sight became a field of blur; shapes sliding down the window in front of me. Nothing but rain everywhere. I fought it for as long as I could, but I can't fight any more. It took everything from me and it will keep taking until there's nothing left of me.

I sat down on the floor, leaned my back against the balcony door, feeling the rain touching my back through the glass. The sound of its tapping somehow became louder. I looked down at the photo again, gasping for your smile. Instead, I realized the frame was wet. Surprised, I let out a strange sound as my throat tightened. The tears streamed down my face and the rain within claimed me, as it did everything else.

Bunker IV

Stephen

*** National Emergency Command and Control ***
***RECC1 London – Online ***
***RECC2 Birmingham – Online ***
RECC3 Shireham – Online
RECC4 Leeds – Online
RECC5 Glasgow – Online – Yarr Ya Fuckers! Anonymous Rules!!
***RECC6 Berrenton – Offline …..

MARY – This book is bloody useless.

COLIN – Yeah, I couldn't understand it either.

MARY – Doesn't matter if I can or can't its covered in coffee!

She is holding the dogeared manual in front of her with a thumb and forefinger.

MARY – Most of the pages are stuck together

COLIN – That wasn't me!

MARY – What?

COLIN – Nothing.

MARY – You mean you didn't spill coffee on it?

COLIN – Erm…

MARY – This can't be the only one in here,

COLIN – Er…

Mary attempts to peel open the book. Large sections of it are now seemingly welded together.

MARY – Where did you find this one?

COLIN – Um…

We are perhaps not seeing Colin in the best light. You may think its because he is stoned out of his brains on super-powerful hydroponic weed. But actually there is a little more going on behind his slightly bloodshot eyes. Colin is calculating. He had of course always known that his little underground paradise couldn't last forever. Now he is trying to assimilate his new guests into the picture. He is possibly, well, no, *definitely*, the only one who couldn't care less about being locked in. Indeed, he hasn't even considered whether or not it's just a huge mistake.

MARY – Colin! Snap out of it, where did you find it?

COLIN – Oh, well, the library.

MARY – Well come on then.

Elsewhere Desmond and Howard are exploring.

DESMOND – I am the senior representative of the civil authority.

HOWARD – Nonsense, I'm the senior military man here, and as this is clearly a martial law situation, the military takes command.

DESMOND – Yes but…. Hang on, you're not military, you're a council employee.

HOWARD – I can be recalled in times of national emergency, and if this is a national emergency then I'm the ranking military in this place.

DESMOND – Even if that were true and we don't know that it is, you'd have to be recalled, and you haven't been have you?

At this point they both enter the First Class living quarters. This is a large, three story room. Circular, going up in three tiers it has a small park in the middle of it with a rather dismal looking tree. Around the park are some shuttered windows in the style of a small shopping precinct. These are in fact part of the Bunker's extensive resource management system. The next tier up has the housing for the senior officers and critical personnel. And then the final tier contains the Senior Officer's living quarters. A rather grand affair with a large window looking out over the plaza.

Scattered about the area are numerous monitors, all showing the Playstation screensaver that is slightly distorted by the ancient CRTs.

Desmond, with his unerring instinct for the trappings of power, heads up to the Senior Officer's rooms. As he enters, the lights come on and he chooses to take this as a good sign. The room itself is, well, ok it's a sixties shag pad. It even has a few of those weird white ball chairs that can't possibly be comfortable to sit in. It too has a monitor but this one is currently blank. Nosing around Desmond finds himself in the Senior Officer's private office. Acting more out of habit than anything else he picks up the red phone and is quite shocked to hear a dialling tone. His first thought is to ring home. But as he dials using the old rotary dialler he realises that he does not want to explain himself to his wife quite yet. He stops and then dials nine, nine, nine. No response.

He sits in the SO's high backed leather chair and has a good old-fashioned think. He looks down at the drawers on either side of the desk. On his first attempt he finds what looks like a pager on a lanyard. On it on one side is the legend 'Senior Officer ' and on the other 'NECC.'

Howard too has an instinct. His instinct leads him to the small security office off the main parkway. This is every bit as drab as you would expect and is mostly still covered in plastic wrapping. Delighted he begins to hunt for what he knows must be there and finds it in very short order. A large locked cabinet. After a moments frustration trying to force it open, on a whim he keys his Berrenton employee security code into the lock keypad and is delighted when it opens. Carefully, lovingly even, he removes an MP5 and checks the chamber.

HOWARD – Now we'll see who's got military authority.

A little more Bunker description. The Library. It is possibly the least b-movie hi-tech room in the building. Indeed it's possible to imagine you have walked into an industrial revolution municipal library. In place of windows various artworks have been placed, both replica and in a few cases original. The residents of Berrenton may even recognize much of it as many of the fixtures, fittings and artworks were previously in the old town hall, including some luxurious leather armchairs.

Mary has quite a task ahead of her. Picture a montage. Mary, busy reading and making notes. Colin, busy rolling and smoking. Howard, carefully stroking his new weapon. Desmond, sitting in the senior officer's chair with his feet up on the table.

So let us be clear. Mary will of course find what she needs to know and when the four gather will be able to reset the system and create a new senior officer. Desmond is now in possession of the senior officer's control key, actually more of a secure device. It will enable the senior officer to open the doors, or indeed anything he wishes as regards the Bunker's command system. Howard has a gun. And Colin couldn't care less about any of it. He will change his mind soon enough.

The kneeling soldier

John

The Reverend Thomas Halliday – a 19th Century folklorist – notes in his book *Folklore of The Lakelands*,

'A curious incident, said to have taken place in the Westmorland town of _____ in 1812; in the Cemetery of the church of St Mungos in the town.

The incumbent of the time – the Revd Thaddaeus Gillton – noted in his diary for August 16th:

"As I left the church to return home this evening I noted the sound of a man weeping to my left. Upon turning I saw a Trooper kneeling upon a patch of grass, obviously overcome with grief. With my own son William serving in Spain I was minded to comfort the young man. However as I approached I noticed that he knelt not beside a grave – as I had supposed – but simply a patch of the area not yet used.

"Upon enquiry, the young man replied that we wept for his 'Manda, from whom he had been parted these long months – but that they would be together that very night. Taking this to mean that he was to visit his love I wished him Godspeed, and expressed a hope that his reunion would be a joyous one; and continued upon my way".

In his diary for the following day The Revd Gillton wrote:

"I have been informed this very morning of the death last night of Amanda Arkwright, daughter of Thomas and Lucinda and spinster of this Parish. It seems that she collapsed and fell into a swoon upon the receipt of a letter (which told her that a soldier to whom she was engaged had been reported killed several weeks previously whilst taking part in a battle) and died within the hour. Thinking perhaps that the soldier I had seen yesterday evening may have imparted such tragic news I hastened to the House of Mr Arkwright. However it seems that no soldier had visited them yesterday. Asking if Amanda had any keepsake of her love, a locket containing a miniature of him was passed to me."

"My surprise was great when I saw the picture, as the image matched my recollection of the soldier I had seen. So shaken was I that I enquired if perhaps they knew if he had a brother; and once again paled upon the news that he was an only child. Making my excuses I fled with speed home to write down these brief words. I will not ask the Sexton where Amanda will be buried, I shall wait and see."

The reverend's final entry on this matter was a short note dated five days later. In it he states that Amanda Arkwright was laid to rest, at the spot where he had seen the kneeling soldier. I have spoken to the current incumbent of St Mungos, and he confirms that there is indeed a headstone dated 1812 for Miss Amanda Arkwright, and beside it is a further one for one Lieutenant Henry Wallashaw – inscribed as serving in the Peninsular war, killed at the Battle of Salamanca. As to the diary, I have no reason to doubt the veracity of the information, which seems so complete and honest in all other matters within.'

Bad Dreams

Clive

I

Standing on the corner of the road were my friends Mike and Chris and James, and a little boy I didn't know. I pulled up alongside them and wound down the window. 'You waiting for a taxi home or something?' quoth I.

'Yup.'

'Hop in. I'll take you. You're more or less on my way.'

'Thanks!'

So off we set. First Mike's place. Little boy still sitting there. Then Chris's. Little boy still sitting there. Finally James's. There I am expecting the little boy to get out with someone, but no.

'Who's the little boy?'

'I don't know,' quoth James.

Oh gawd! Each of us had assumed that one or more of the others knew who he was.

'Where do you live?'

'Blackheath.'

Well, there are Blackheaths all over the place, but none of them anywhere near here, and can I get any more sense out of him than that? Not a chance.

I remember a time when in such circumstances one would have taken him to the nearest police station and let them sort it out, but only a fool would do that nowadays. The only sensible thing to do is to leave him by the side of the road and let someone else find him. But how can you possibly do that?

II

We could see each other, forty feet away across the crowd, but if we descended into that milling throng, we'd never find each other. Would my phone work in that place? I knew the number of the announcer; it was worth a try. Would they be too busy to take my call? I gestured to her to indicate what I was trying to do.

The phone worked. The announcement came. It was like a dream. The crowd parted like the Red Sea, and she ran across to me. The Red Sea closed behind her and continued on its various hurrying ways.

I held her close for a few minutes, then she reached up and kissed my tear stained cheek, pulled away from me, and disappeared into the chaos. I never saw her again.

III

Percy suddenly decided that he was going to come with us, after all. He started to put his boots on, but then realized that his Mum was already quite a long way up the road, and set off at a run, one foot padding along in a sock, and the other thumping along in a boot, laces flying loose.

I slowed down and let Bev get ahead a bit. As I'd expected, Percy overtook me without a glance, and I dashed back to pick up his other boot. It had a toy iron in it.

When he originally said he wasn't coming, Bev had told him, "That's okay. Auntie Sharon will be very happy to have you here. We'll be popping in in a week's time to pick up the rest of our stuff, and you can come then if you've changed your mind."

I hoped we'd got everything we needed for that first week, but I was far from confident. I knew we'd not thought about it nearly carefully enough, and was sure we'd forgotten something. I was right: we arrived at the car, which we'd loaded with all the less valuable stuff the previous day – and discovered I didn't have the car key. I put down my rucksack, and Percy's boot, and ran back again.

Sharon met me at the door with the key, laughing fit to bust. "Have you got a spare sock for Percy? He must have worn holes in that one!"

"Probably. Somewhere. He'll survive."

As I reached the collapsed section of the road for the third time, another huge chunk of the cliff broke away. I watched it fall, seemingly in slow motion, then heard it crash into the sea far below, a long drawn-out crashing, thundering sound.

God, thank goodness none of us were on that, I thought. I detoured even further across the field than we had before, keeping a long way back from the edge, and thanked our lucky stars that we'd had the foresight to leave the car so much further up the road.

IV

Have you ever tried to take in sail manually on a fifteen metre cat in a storm in the dark? Don't. Well, don't let yourself get into a situation where you have to. If you've got to do it, you've got to do it. And to think there used to be folks who sailed these things just for the fun of it!

We were tacking, beating upwind. It was blowing a good stiff breeze, white horses just catching the last of the light, but it hadn't been blowing long and the sea hadn't got up much. Dark and threatening with heavy clouds, but we'd got plenty of sea room and we weren't worried. She was wide and stable, so we were flying along under full sail.

Then the rain hit us, and big squalls. No surprise there, of course. The waves began to get bigger, and she began to jump about a bit. Still no surprise, but Chris sensibly decided it was time to roll in a bit of sail. She spilt the wind and hit the button. Whirr – phht – whirr – phht – silence. And the lights had gone out in the cabin, too. We didn't know exactly what had failed in the electrics, but something had.

In the dark I scrabbled in the locker under the cockpit seat and found the little handle to wind the sail in manually. I hooked myself onto the safety line and scrambled up onto the cabin roof to the foot of the mast. Fitted the handle into the socket in the boom and wound like there was no tomorrow. Then the sail stuck – something jammed in the boom? In the dark and the pouring rain, I couldn't see what was wrong. I inched my way along the boom to try to find the problem, but the boom was swinging about and even with a sand-textured finish, the top of the cabin was slippery in the wet. A moment later I was in the drink.

I'd got a lifejacket on, of course, and I was on a safety line. But it's still no fun. It's still damn cold, and you still breathe a lot of water. And it seemed to be ages before Chris was hauling me back into the cockpit.

And we still had three-quarters of a sail up, and it was developing into a real storm. What now? We were very afraid the mast was going to break, and then we'd be drifting and lucky to be found in time. We could cut the sail loose and save the mast, but then we'd be drifting anyway. We just hoped against hope that the mast would survive the storm.

V

We arrived at the house a little before dawn. The house had retained some heat from the previous afternoon. Even without a fire in the grate, it was warmer inside than out – well, less bitterly cold anyway. We searched all around the house, inside and out, for anything to burn. There wasn't much, and most of what there was was too damp. It wouldn't dry out, even inside the house beside whatever fire we could make, in time to be any use to us.

In particular, we couldn't find anything at all that would burn easily enough to get a fire started.

We just had to huddle together to try to keep warm. Sleep was out of the question.

But sleep we did. When I woke, the sun was streaming in through the window, and my feet, in a patch of sunshine, actually felt warm. Jackie was snoring, but Chris was awake. She'd managed to get a fire going somehow, and was cooking the rabbit we'd snared the previous day. She'd found some potatoes growing in a patch not far from the house as well.

'There's a spring at the foot of the cliff over there. Looks like good water. I've washed and had a drink. I can't find anything to boil any water in though, so there's going to be no tea I'm afraid.'

I thought that was just a joke – we'd not had any tea for a week. But she'd found a packet of tea in a cupboard.

VI

There was a lot of traffic. The rain began to get heavier, and got very heavy. I slowed down a lot. Most others didn't.

I kept a good braking distance from the vehicle in front. People overtaking me, probably scared witless by the idiots two car lengths behind them, kept pulling into the space I'd left, as they do. I kept dropping back, trying to preserve my braking space, as I do. The result was that I was going even more slowly than I would otherwise have felt the need to, but so be it.

The inevitable happened, of course. I was able to stop before hitting the mess, and got myself onto the hard shoulder in the hope that I might escape the impact of following traffic. Not being very confident of that, I got out of the passenger side of the car, and legged it up the embankment.

For a short while I watched the mayhem from the top of the bank. I watched as the pile-up grew. My car seemed to lead a charmed life there on the hard shoulder – the whole road was full of carnage, and it spilled onto the hard shoulder both in front of and behind my car, but my car was untouched.

Then I watched in horror as two big trucks, side by side, attempted to stop before hitting the pile. They slid sideways into it, and a third slammed straight on into the side of them. The first was a fuel tanker, followed by a liquid oxygen tanker. And something burst into flame.

I didn't wait to watch any longer. I wondered how far I could get before the first of the two tanks burst in the heat, and worse than that, the second as well. I ran, looking all the while for anywhere that would give me some shelter from the blast I knew was likely any time. A dip in the ground, anything.

They found me two hundred yards from the road. How much of that I'd run, and how much I'd flown, no-one will ever know. I was lucky they found me – I could have died of hypothermia so easily, lying battered and unconscious in a field in the rain like that. I was the only survivor of the accident, and they still don't know exactly how many people died in it.

VII

One day I'm going about my normal life – then the next thing I remember, I'm in here.

Have I done something dreadful? If so, I don't remember a thing about it, and I've never had any intention of doing anything bad. I don't remember any court case, nothing.

It's not really much like a prison, anyway. Fenced all around, but not at all secure, and no guards or anything – not as far as I've seen. But we're all wearing painfully brightly coloured boiler suits, and all the other inmates are shuffling zombies. At least I'm not a shuffling zombie.

Well – I don't feel like a shuffling zombie. I wonder whether the others feel like shuffling zombies? They look like shuffling zombies to me. I wonder whether I look like a shuffling zombie to everyone else?

I could vault that fence easily. I suppose it would keep the shuffling zombies in well enough. Well, I think I could vault it easily – as long as I'm still not a shuffling zombie in reality. Would something dreadful happen to me if I tried to make my escape?

What will happen to me if I don't try to make my escape? Horror of horrors, perhaps a few days of whatever we're given to eat here – we must get something to eat! – will turn me into a shuffling zombie.

So there's nothing to lose.

And yes, I'm right, I can vault that fence easily. And nothing dreadful – nothing at all – has happened to me yet. Now where to go?

From being in what was virtually a field, I'm rapidly in a maze of ancient narrow streets – deserted for the moment, but looking as though they were busy last night, and probably will be again quite soon, when the sun comes up. This orange boiler suit is a bit of a problem. And all I've got under it, I find, is a pair of orange underpants and an orange vest. I wonder whether the locals – any of them – might be sympathetic to my plight? Or whether they'll simply turn me over to the authorities?

Upon Insanity

Jack

Are you mad?

Are you. Mad?

It's something a madman once asked me.

"Of course not."

"You're lying." he grins. spinning the knife in his hands. The oscillating blade flashes, reflecting the light from the fire.

"I'm not. I'm as sane as the next man."

"But how sane is the next man? Or the man after that? Or any of the men before? Never mind that, how sane are the women?"

"What?"

He laughs, and tosses the blade. It flicks high into the air, and my eyes are drawn to it. One, two, three rotations. He catches it deftly. It never stops moving.

"What's madness?" he asks.

"You."

He wags a finger, tipping his hat at an angle. "Not so. It's myriad. It might be scientific, illnesses in our brains. Neurons misfiring. Dots not connecting. Chemicals not reacting. Or all of those things happening, but in the wrong places. Or maybe it's a sickness of our souls, a mangling of the moralities in the ghosts in our machines. I don't know; I am not mad. My head is clear as day. As the birds in the sky, or the fish in the river. I see them swimming, little swishes of their tails, moving them forward. Swish, swish, swish."

"I – "

"Bloop."

I frown, as he cackles again.

"Of course you are mad. If you are not, how do you explain the pictures in your head? When you sleep. The faces of people you know, or those you've never met, straying into surreal situations, or consorting with confuddling creatures. Portraying powers that shouldn't be possible. Places you've been, their realities warped, only just recognisable as things you know, but twisted by the boundless stretches of your own imagination. Do you not dream?"

I nod.

"And are they not strange?"

"Well...yes."

He laughs delightedly. "Therefore you are mad. There is a little bit of madness in us all. Without insanity, we could not be human. We would be identical, functionless machines. Oh, speaking of which. A walking train."

He points with his knife, and I look. He's not lying.

It saunters along the tracks, clicking its boots merrily. Steam puffs from its giant chimney, and its bright yellow body is streaked with dust. Ten massive, trousered legs propel it along its rough path, carrying the train at least eight feet from the ground. Its feet pat with a keen rhythm, and every so often a cheerful toot erupts from its front carriage. It trails the rest of the procession behind it, the dull brown compartments bouncing along like tin cans on a string.

"Nice trousers." I admit grudgingly.

"Thank you, you're very kind." whistles the train, not breaking its impressive pace.

We watch it crash through a border crossing, heading for the ocean.

"Such a shame," the madman shakes his head, "that people only get glimpses of their own madness. And barely ever remember them. You are far more lucky."

"So is this a dream?" I ask, rapping my fingers curiously against the window of the car. The contact causes ripples, flowing slowly outward like those of a stone in a lake. Out of the corner of my eye, I can see my long-dead grandfather salute me from the back seat.

"Of course this isn't a dream." snaps the man. "What a crazy thing to suggest. You don't dream. You wake up, and you remember one. That's it. You can't ever experience a dream. This...this is so much better than that."

A baby bottle suddenly bounces off the window, making me jump.

"Stop the car!" I yell.

"Who are you talking to?" the man asks.

I suddenly realized he's not driving, and there is no car. I'm stood on the corner of the pavement, staring at a sensible brick structure. I know where we are. This is Egham station. But it's warped, like the man had said. I can see it clearly, but the dimensions are all different. I raise a finger, tracing the edge of the track out of the station as it curves away from me, stretching around a distant bend that I know shouldn't exist. But I don't know why I know that. Another train skitters around the bend as I watch, gaining speed as it patters into the station. Hordes of faceless people cheer as the new train bends its knees level with the platform, and they pile on.

The tap on the shoulder makes me jump. It's Robert Webb. I turn to see earnest eyes, and a pleasant smile. Over his shoulder, I can see the building site; cranes disappear into the clouds, and masses of sand are dredged across the green pavement. It makes that short street seem much larger than I know it used to be.

"Excuse me." says Webb. "David and I – "he gestures over his shoulder, where a skeletally thin Mitchell waves politely at me, "are here to fight zombies."

I frown. "What with?"

"This fish." he answers, gesturing to the haddock flapping futilely on the ground.

He scowls at the sound of my laughter.

"It's not funny." he says. "This is a very deadly fish."

Behind him, David Mitchell nods seriously.

I walk to the building site, the pair of them at my shoulder. Putting my hardhat on, I hear a shout come from somewhere far above us. Mitchell and Webb step neatly apart as a great cascade of sand pools on the concrete at our feet.

"I'm sorry for laughing." I say. "But there aren't any zombies here."

They raise their eyebrows, confused.

"Of course there are." says Webb. "There's one over there."

He points.

The fat zombie stands with its back to us, two thick tree-stump legs parked on the narrow girder, looking out to the sea. The steel is short and wide, allowing plenty of room for the creature's heavy feet, and coloured with a purple tinge. Vague patterns flow through it, circles and squares and triangles all colliding and coalescing into each other with the grace of agile, living things. I stare, transfixed, until the nausea starts in the pit of my stomach and the bile rises in my throat. The steel ends abruptly a little way past the creature, burrowing into a gigantic black obelisk. The massive structure looms far above the zombie, its peak disappearing into the clouds. Waves crash against its broad base, and the thing on the girder angles its gruesome head downwards to stare. It looks especially obscene against the bright blue of the sky behind it, and the mysterious majesty of the obelisk. As if someone had lobbed a handful of red-flecked mud against a carefully painted landscape.

Without warning, a wave slams against the foundations below, sending up a huge gush of spray. The zombie moans and turns its head away instinctively, and in that instant, it sees me.

It squeals, pumping its chunky legs into a frenzy, achieving a speed I wouldn't have thought possible for its size. I turn and slam my fist on the door, my eyes finding David Mitchell's, gazing curiously from behind it.

"Let me in." I beg.

He shakes his head.

I pound on the door. It doesn't budge.

"Please."

"Nope." he says firmly, with the academic authority that comes across so well in his panel shows. "We've changed our minds."

I don't scream as I face the demon rushing towards me.

Now that it's closer, I can see its twisted, elongated jaw, and the blood on its outstretched fingers. The t-shirt it wears is in tatters, and the zombie's stomach bulges alarmingly. I can hear the chatters of the many tiny, vicious little things it contains, and for the second time in as many minutes I almost throw up. I look for a weapon, but there's nothing anywhere near me on the girder, and Mitchell has left the door firmly locked behind me. I know that even if I could find a weapon, to puncture the zombie's stomach would be death – the tiny abominations would swarm me. The zombie is closer now, rushing past the others – how had I not seen all the others? – and I can hear the snapping of its jaw, and see the terrifying hunger in its eyes. Instinctively, I raise my plasma cutter, and shoot a thin line of fire directly at its knee.

The flesh squelches as the flames tear into it, and the zombie screeches as the leg is torn away. It slips, meeting the girder with a loud clang, and both parts of the creature plunge into the sea below.

I stare at the cutter in my hand.

How do I have control over this?

Am I insane?

The others race towards me, the combinations of their hideous idiosyncrasies blending together until I can't see them as separate beings, only a single snowballing maelstrom of horror, gathering speed as it rattles towards me.

I know what I can do.

I close my eyes, and concentrate.

When I open them, it is early morning, and I'm standing in a deserted street in the middle of Manchester. This one is especially odd. Not because of its proportions – the buildings seem normal sized. Blurred but otherwise unremarkable posters litter the walls. Not because of its inhabitants – there are none. It's early in the morning, perhaps 7am. The sun is shining hopefully, and frost has gathered on the windows. It's exactly as I remember it. That's at once the most comforting, and the most frightening thing.

I'm never going to find my purple jukebox here, I realise.

My legs burn as I pedal frantically up and down the streets. Nothing even closely resembling a music shop jumps out at me. Near one of the universities I spot a jukebox, but it's not purple. I shout in frustration.

Purple's the one I want.

"Are you mad?"

I spin, almost falling off the bike.

That same man is there again.

"Who are you?" he asks, spinning a knife in his hand.

"Me?"

"You're mad."

"I'm as sane as the next man."

He gestured around him, at the wide, sparse streets.

"But isn't this strange?"

"No, it's real."

He laughed, a long, high giggle.

"Everything you see is real. It's just been strangely put together. Did you know; our brains can't construct faces from scratch? Everyone you meet here, you've seen before, in some way or another. Their surroundings are more...malleable. Malleable."

He rolled the word around in his mouth, as if tasting a fine wine.

"Truth is stranger than fiction, and fiction is created from truth. And if the fiction is created from the truth, then either the fiction must be somewhat true or the truth must be somewhat fiction. You follow, yes? Normality only exists as it's created by us. We say what's normal. So who's to say what's real?"

"Are you real?"

He laughed. "You'd be mad to think I'm not real."

The man – the madman (or just the man) – straightened his jacket. The knife has vanished.

"Come on." he said. "We have to see Matt Damon about your jukebox."

He turned on his heel, and opened the door of the gym behind him. I follow him, my mouth dropping open in wonder. I'm on the edge of a cliff, towering hundreds of feet above a grey mass of fog that obscures much of the calm ocean below us.

Out beyond the cliffs, against the backdrop of a lime-green sky, a city waits, floating serenely above the blue water. The buildings aren't like any I remember seeing before – jagged edges reach towards the clouds, and clumps of soil tumble off the chunks of land that inexplicably suspend them in the air. Many of them are half-built, their steel, meshed frames visible through the outer masonry. The metropolis stretches for miles, far farther than I could see. Dark, spherical vehicles flicker between the spires, scurrying and swarming like insects. I can't see anything besides air, earth and metal amongst the buildings, but I know that the creatures living there aren't human. They're aliens from some distant planet, and either they've come to me, or I've come to them.

In the centre, an immense tower rises from the ground like a nail from a puddle. It has only two distinct sides, with its foundations apparently built on the shape of a giant, thin oval. Like the other structures, it has no doors or windows, or any other aspects that might normally define architecture in the world I'm used to. I can only see one dark, blank facet, glowing faintly green with a mysterious energy. It fills my vision as we get closer, and I stare at the huge central spire as we circle it. I can feel the man at my shoulder, and I know something is wrong.

This shouldn't be here.

We spiral higher around the nameless tower, with the structures surrounding it fading into the mist like anthills.

Our craft – my craft – passes briefly through a cloud. I turn to stare outwards, back to the landmass we came from. It is wide and unremarkable. And so very far away.

I ask the question aloud; although I'm not sure the man is even there anymore.

"Is this real?"

I lean forward, and tumble from the machine. The tower is gone. As is the city below it. The sky is no longer green. There is only a grey blanket of fog, rushing up to greet me.

Is this a dream? Am I insane?

The fog envelops me.

We'll soon find out.

Bunker – Digression

Stephen

As the four Bunker residents head for the Command chair to have a full and frank exchange of views we will consider the minds of the people who built it.

The bunker had originally been conceived during the second world war. Then it had been a massive series of bunkers stretching across the island connected by a network of underground pneumatic trains. This had been smiled on by Churchill. At least that's what its designer had been told, laughed at would have been more accurate.

But the plans stayed on file, as civil service plans are wont to do, and when in the fifties the fear of Armageddon raised its head, they were dug out. Upon review it was decided that they were perhaps a little over the top. The first idea that was scrapped was actually connecting them all. Then the sheer number was reduced. Even with these changes the cost would be astronomical and Britain's finances had hardly been what you might call fluid in those post war days. But quietly and under the cover of an equally secret but not quite as top secret nuclear bunker plan, the NECC broke ground.

But the problem with building top secret buildings, especially underground, in the middle of active cities is that its unbelievably expensive. You should, when you read 'unbelievably,' stress each syllable. Despite what many conspiracy theorists will tell you, funnelling vast sums of money leaves a trace. And it needs to be a huge sum if when it reaches the pockets of the people doing the work you want it to remain silent. It was incidentally this need for penny pinching that led to RECC6 having a hydroelectric plant and not a nuclear one. In fact it was the possibility of doing this that led to the Berrenton site being selected.

A breakthrough came in 1960. After what turned out to be a massive con on the part of the British government, the Americans finally came to the table to discuss nukes. They agreed to scrap Blue Streak, their own system, and let the American forces put their system on board both British soil and British subs. This was a multi-level deal. On the surface, they were purchasing the equipment. But actually it was more like renting out space. They could launch them, but only with the permission of their real owners. In return for this the Americans agreed to both let the British claim that they had in fact bought them and were now a nuclear power and pay. In turn the MOD was able to funnel all the money it was supposedly spending on the nukes into the NECC, as well as the not so modest sum that was being charged as part of the rental agreement.

Suddenly the NECC was flooded with money. Drowned in it even. Serious discussion was had regarding the deep underground train system that had been scrapped. What had been a traditionally sedate British system suddenly had the money to make things actually tolerable. On staff psychologists were shocked to suddenly be listened to as their suggestion that 'Twenty years is a long time, perhaps we should think about mental well being?' was now being considered. Room for recreation was allotted and building commenced. Most notably, in the case of RECC1 resulting in a cricket pitch.

Sadly, RECC6 was the last Bunker to be completed. More fortunate than RECC7 that remains a dank hole in the ground, true, but that initial flush of spending had reduced somewhat when it came to RECC6. But we can at least be thankful that our four residents will have opportunities to rest and relax in an environment designed to reduce the 'cabin fever' that would be inevitable in a long stay. Albeit an environment designed in the sixties…

Three Sons

Rosie

I had three sons, and outlived them all. They all died in battle within a few days of one another. I received all three telegrams at the same time.

I mourned the eldest then. I'd mourned the others sooner.

The eldest was conscripted. I cried the day he received his conscription papers. I cried the day I got the telegram telling me he'd been killed. I'm crying still.

The second was also conscripted. I cried the day he received his conscription papers. He died to me the day I received his letter telling me proudly how he'd killed a man. I mourned him then.

The youngest died to me the day he joined the army. He was a volunteer.

Bunker V

Stephen

MARY – What do you mean 'No Decaff'?

COLIN – Well I'm not sure, but I've been over the beverages section of the supplies catalogue and I don't remember feeling that sense of sick dread I feel when I read that word so, no, no decaff.

Mary stops dead and turns to face Colin.

MARY – What about humus?

COLIN – Dunno, never looked. But I'd imagine there's a decent stock of chick peas around here somewhere.

MARY – This place is going to be hell as it is. If I can't chill out with some humus, carrot sticks and wine then things are going to get impossible.

COLIN – Ahh well, carrots and wine. No problem. I can grow carrots and as for wine, gallons of the stuff.

Slightly mollified, Mary begins walking again.

MARY – The sooner we are out of here the better. No way can I survive with three walking bollocks as company.

COLIN – So you still think this is all a mistake then?

MARY – Considering the alternative?? Damn right I think this is a mistake.

COLIN – Well we can't turn on the systems to check the status…

Mary, who has been working on nothing but for the last however many hours, stops once more to favour Colin with a dirty look.

COLIN – But… what if we could get a wireless signal?

MARY – First thing I tried.

COLIN – Well yeah, but you tried deep inside this place. There is one place that's a little closer to the surface and a little less thickly covered.

MARY – Colin, we've been down here hours. Why didn't you mention this earlier?

A lesser man would be fooled by her sweet demeanour. But Colin is a little more wise than he lets on. First, he takes a few steps back.

COLIN – The air reclamation units are closer to the surface, and if you put your phone on the metal cowling you can sometimes pick up a signal.

MARY takes a meaningful step forwards.

COLIN – But not all the time, depends on… stuff. But sometimes…..

Mary takes a moment to consider the factors. On the one hand should she just punch Colin now? Perhaps not. On the other is it worth checking this new potential source of information out? She certainly feels it would be useful to know what's going on before deciding who gets the command chair. If it's only a few minutes then it doesn't matter. If it's a genuine apocalypse and they are stuck down there forever, then who gets the chair is *way* more important. If for no other reason, she has discovered, than that the Commander has the final decision on a death penalty decision. Not that she thinks any one currently in the Bunker would have the balls to do that, but she does think if anyone should then it really should be her.

MARY – How 'Not all the time'?

COLIN – I dunno, sometimes I can hook a signal, others I can't.

MARY – So if we don't get a signal it could either be because life as we know it has ended or it could be because the wind isn't blowing in the right direction?

COLIN – Well, yeah, but… worth a try?

Mary considers this for a moment then gives firm nod.

MARY – Yeah, worth a try.

She motions with a hand for Colin to lead on which he is, for the moment, happy to do.

Back in the Command centre Howard and Desmond have discovered further causes of dispute.

DESMOND – Look, all I'm saying is even if there was a reason to fire the damn thing what if you miss? Quite apart from hitting an innocent target what about all these ancient electronics?

HOWARD – Then I'd best not miss.

DESMOND – Miss *who*! Theres only three other people in here!

Despite his outward belligerence Howard is wavering. It has occurred to him that maybe the gun was a step too far.

DESMOND – With the greatest respect Howard, what are you going to do with it when the doors open?

This is a damn good question and one that Howard hasn't considered. Like many a gun nut before him, when presented with the opportunity to play with one he took it. But to be fair to Howard he is at least competent to handle it. Imagine if Colin had found the guns? He very deliberately shits the selector to 'Safe' and slings the gun behind him. Thus taking away some of Desmond's concerns if not all of them while at the same time giving him the reassuring weight of the thing.

HOWARD – I still say we should go looking for them, they could be up to anything.

DESMOND – Planning a revolution perhaps? Instead of a coup….

Howard's hand drops back to the gun for a moment, but then he thinks the better of it and instead uses a finger to pontificate.

HOWARD – That little sod has been down here for god knows how long. Long enough to rewire the place at least. Maybe he knows a way out? They could be upstairs laughing at us as we speak.

DESMOND – I hardly think Mary would leave me down here with…. with no hope of escape.

Howard notes the lame ending to that particular sentence but rises above it.

HOWARD – You've got that security thing, lets go to the doors and see if there is somewhere we can plug it in?

Desmond considers this for a moment. It's not a terrible idea, but he'd rather not admit it.

DESMOND – Ok, but I have a condition.

HOWARD – Whats that?

DESMOND – When we get there no trying to shoot out the lock.

Very large chunks of the Bunker are taken up by equipment. One whole floor for example is given over to the Bunker Super Computer. I'll let you take that in for a moment. But by far the two largest lumps of machinery are the waste reclamation system and the air reclamation system. In fact the two areas neatly sandwich the rest of the Bunker. Although in fairness the waste reclamation system also includes the hydro plant. Realistically speaking even if the base were full to the brim with humans it would still only mean that twenty percent of it was for day to day human activity. The vast majority of the machinery was designed not only with numerous back ups in case of failure but also to not be interfered with unless absolutely necessary.

Now, what Colin doesn't know is that the first thing to happen upon sealing the Bunker was that the external air supply is shut down and internal supplies relied upon for as long as is possible. Also, the external system is connected to several monitors that check the air for pollutants. The system then decides on any given day if it's going to breath or not. It's when the system is shut that Colin's little trick works. Mind you, even if he knew this he would be unable to explain why.

MARY – So I just put it on here?

Colin nods, although not very enthusiastically.

Mary carefully places her phone on a nondescript cowling. She fiddles through a few menus and is eventually able to force it to search for a connection. Then she waits, her arms folded. Colin continues to fidget on the spot.

After a shockingly short amount of time the phone finds something.

NEBS-NATIONAL EMERGENCY BROADCAST SYSTEM-SIGNAL STRENGTH 1 – Password Protected.

MARY – What?? password protected?

The reality of what she has read then dawns on her.

MARY – Emergency Broadcast? Could that be part of the Bunker? Transmitting on auto because the doors are shut?

Colin shrugs, torn between being glad his trick worked and wary over what Mary's response will be.

MARY – FUCK!

The main door to the Bunker is an impressive sight. But despite a desperate fingertip search of its vastness neither Howard nor Desmond can find anything resembling a key hole or even a housing for the device.

HOWARD – Wave it around the door, maybe it's wireless or Bluetooth.

DESMOND – I think this predates either of those technologies.

HOWARD – A remote control then? Point and press.

DESMOND – At what? And with what? This isn't a damn tricorder you know.

HOWARD – What?

DESMOND – Oh never mind. Lets get back to the Control Room. Hopefully the other two have had better luck than us.

HOWARD – No matter what happens that little stoner has got to be put in his place. Trespass, theft, drugs. He needs to be dealt with.

DESMOND – A job for the authorities I think Howard.

HOWARD – Yes, but if we are stuck in here then that's us isn't it?

The Fish and the Bicycle

Clive

Simon skipped breakfast that morning. He cleaned his teeth, swallowed a glass of water, and set off before dawn, pushing his bicycle the five miles into the village. He arrived long before Sushila's father opened the shop, but he knew that if he banged on the shutters someone would ask who it was, and he knew they wouldn't turn him away.

Sushila answered, and her big brother Premdas mended his chain for him cheerfully enough. "That's the third time in less than two weeks, Simon. You really need a new chain – and you should change the sprocket and the chain wheel too, they're terribly worn and they'll spoil your new chain if you don't."

Simon knew Premdas was right, and wasn't just trying to make a few extra rupees out of him. But how could he afford the 280 rupees? Even just a new chain would stretch his budget, but how often was he shelling out three rupees to have his chain fixed? And it always broke at the most inconvenient times, too.

He thanked Premdas, and then cycled back past his house to the little cove where he kept his canoe. He hid his bicycle behind the usual rock, and paddled out to sea for the morning's fishing.

It wasn't a good morning. By eleven o'clock – at a guess – he hadn't caught anything. For the thousandth time, he cursed the big boats further offshore that were sweeping the sea clean of fish. He remembered how, before they came, he could fill the bottom of his canoe in an hour or two.

Then he struck lucky. It was a big one. Once he got it on board, he could see just how big it was. Curled right round, it only just fit in his jhola. It must have weighed at least five or six kilo – enough to pay for a new chain, chainwheel and sprocket – very nearly. He knew Sushila's father would lend him the rest.

He set off back to the shore in high spirits. He pulled his canoe above the high water mark, and ran behind the rock to get his bicycle.

It had gone.

He was sure that someone had simply borrowed it, and that he'd get it back all right; but in the meantime, how could he get to the market in the village before his fish went off in that heat?

What use is a fish without a bicycle?

(Also published in *The Reminiscences of Penny Lane*.)

The Headless Stag of Wearning Chase

John

In 1765 a story was published in *The Gentlemen's Enquerry Periodical* of an odd occurrence that had taken place the previous winter, in Herefordshire.

A certain gentleman, Donald Richwell of the manor of Wearning was returning from visiting his good friend and neighbour Michael Trevalant, following the path through the open woodlands adjacent to Wearning. However, as the track turned towards his house he heard what he described as an "unearthly howling" coming from the woodlands.

His horse – normally the most placid of beasts – reared and threw him, and galloped off in a panic. Richwell landed in a ditch; but as he was about to rise, soaking wet and covered in mud, he spied a fantastical procession leaving the woodland.

Leading the procession was a large bearded man with a garland of holly leaves upon his brow, and dressed in a purple leather coat with bright gold buttons. He rode a piebald shire horse whose eyes appeared to glow with a pale green luminescence.

Following him rode a motley crew of vagabonds, all of them dressed in rags that were obviously once bright and colourful garments – although the style of them was hundreds of years old. Each figure had a vacant expression upon their face, yet their mouths were open wide, and from within came the eerie howling

Richwell had first heard. Upon each figure's chest was a sigil, the heraldry of a rearing white stag, with a silver chain around its neck and no head (although the antlers were shown exactly where they should have been had the head been there).

The last human figure was on foot, and held in his hands a silver chain. Being led by the chain was – just as the sigil – a white stag; who trotted along behind, seemingly oblivious to the fact that it had no head...

Fear gripped Richwell, who crouched in that muddy ditch – too scared to move and hoping that this macabre procession would not notice him. However, as the last figure shuffled passed it turned at stared right at him... and it had *his* face!

Richwell was found in the ditch the following morning by his equerry, who had become concerned when they had not returned home. Richwell swore that every detail of this story was true, but claimed that he could not recall anything that had occurred after seeing the figure's face.

Squire Donald Richwell took his own life four weeks later, leaving a note which claimed that he had seen the headless white Stag in the grounds of his house, and thought that the bearded man was coming to claim him for their Grotesque Parade.

*

The House no longer exists, and Wearning Chase is now a commuter belt new town for Hereford. The path where the incident is said to have occurred is now part of a housing estate, and is called White Stag Ride. The White stag has never been seen since.

However, in 1994 there were reports of a large bearded man in a faded purple coat roaming the housing estate at midnight, bawling out what were described as "foreign sounding songs." The police were never able to find the man, and although there were multiple sightings reported, not a single image of the man appeared on any of the CCTV cameras in the estate.

Alex

Merrill

I put the phone down. And I start to cry.

It's the first time I've spoken to Alex in more than two weeks. He's been away with his mother. Italy, they said. It was only for a week. But they had things to deal with, passports to sort out, flights to book. No time for a cursory call to the man who brought him up for ten years.

My life is still bound to Alex in ways I can't even begin to describe. There aren't words in the English language to articulate the bond between father and son. Love. So short a word, and so...insufficient. I love him. Those three words sound so meaningless, so clichéd. They're true, God, they're true. But they're not enough. They don't describe the joy I felt when he was born. The excitement with which I watched him grow up. And the pain I felt when he was taken away from me.

If I'm honest with myself, my marriage to Diane was already falling apart when Alex was born. We had him to try and strengthen it again. That was back when he was just a thing, just a nameless lump. It was a stupid idea, and deep down I think we both knew it. Children don't strengthen marriages without testing them first. I remember we screamed at each other almost as loudly as Alex would scream at us. Neither of us could ever find the time for the baby. That's not to say we didn't love him. (Again, that word.) But we both worked long hours. We had to. If we didn't turn up, we'd get fired. And neither of us could afford to. Another reason why having Alex was a stupid idea. We could barely afford to support ourselves, much less him.

I look up at the wall, to the picture that was taken of the three of us shortly after he was born. We appear a happy, if tired, family. It took us both hours to get Alex into a vaguely presentable state. But the end result was worth it. It's just a pity Diane and I didn't love each other by then. We didn't hate each other. There were no disagreements. But by the time we started trying for Alex, I felt like she was my roommate, rather than my wife. I'd still spend hours in her company. I'd still talk to her about anything. But I just didn't love her in the same way, and she felt the same. When I fell in love with her, it was the happiest time in my life up till then. And when Alex was born, I didn't think there could be anyone else on the planet who was as proud as I was. I had two great times in my life. I'm just sorry the timing was off.

Alex sensed it, as he grew up. All children have abilities to detect that kind of thing, abilities that adults rarely give them credit for. He knew that something was wrong, that Mummy and Daddy didn't act in the same way that the other parents did. They didn't kiss or hug each other. They didn't sleep in a double bed like he'd seen round his friend's houses. They didn't watch TV together. They just exchanged glances, chatted briefly on the landing. Sat in separate rooms, eating in silence, perhaps with a book. He knew.

We weren't unhappy. We'd still share tales of his first steps, still get excited together about his work at school. Break into hysterics at his first words. I'd still happily go back and relive those times that I shared with the two of them. But it wasn't a marriage. Both of us knew that.

There's a painting, framed on my desk. I put it next to the window, so that on a sunny day, the light will shine directly onto it. The bright colours always draw my eyes straight to it, whenever I walk in here. Alex drew it when he was four. They're stick figures. One blue, one red, one green. Labelled Mummy, Daddy, and me. I remember being so thrilled at his handwriting. He hadn't managed to join it up by that time, but it was legible, which is more than you can say for most kids his age. I asked him a question.

Why are we all different colours, Alex?

He looked at me in that way that only children can, as if I was a bit simple. And then he replied.

It's only a drawing, Daddy. Not real life. Why shouldn't we be different colours?

Of all the things he's ever said, that one especially has stuck in my mind. It's a simple enough sentence, one that would make enough sense of any other child. It's logical, it's obvious. But I'm sure there's a gem of philosophy somewhere in there. I'm sure he was trying to tell me something. But I didn't know what. I still don't.

It took us six years. Six years of Alex's life to finally admit we were better off apart. It's true what they say. Don't stick together for the sake of the child. He would have been too young to know what was going on. He wouldn't have been upset. He's an intelligent child, and he's confident. He would have grown up simply knowing that his family were different, and he wouldn't have cared. He would have been happy.

Diane and I stuck together for simple reasons. We'd hoped that Alex would bring us closer together. He didn't. We stayed the same, but now with added responsibilities, and divided emotional loyalties. We stuck together because we were scared, because we weren't sure if we could go it alone.

We had to, eventually. We sat Alex down at the kitchen table, and we explained that Daddy was going to live somewhere else. Did he know what a divorce was?

Yes, he explained. Fred's mummy and daddy got one. Fred was upset for a while.

He wasn't upset. He took the news exactly as I had expected him to. Calmly.

It's not your fault. I remember telling him. A look of confusion crossed his face.

Why is it my fault? he asked.

It was at that point I realised I was going to fuck it up. I was going to cause him emotional damage, simply because I'd been watching too much fucking TV. Taking lines out of the soaps.

Diane took over. I don't remember what she said. I just watched him, his eyes flitting quietly between the two of us. When she had explained all, she asked him if he had any questions. He nodded.

"Can I have a bacon sandwich?"

*

I still phone him. At least once every two days. I used to visit, until Diane started to see other men. She said we'd all be better off if he visited me. That worked fine for me. I managed to find another house almost immediately. Money became less of a problem, now that I was only living for myself. I began to build up decent savings. I could afford to have him over for days at a time.

There was the legal stuff, of course. Separation of affairs. Reminders of my old life. I dealt with them quickly and quietly, with the occasional referral to my solicitor. There was no drama in the breakup between Diane and myself. No arguments, no slammed doors. We just extricated ourselves from each other's lives, and carried on.

I got a new job. More money. I started eating better. Went for a run occasionally. I even started dating for a few horrible misguided weeks. I took up writing. While I was holding that pen, I became someone else. I escaped from my life.

But I did not see my son.

I spoke to him, of course, every day. But when it comes down to it, I'm talking to machine. And when I put the phone down, I'm alone again. I can't touch him, I can't hold him. I can't see him.

I lean back in my chair, in a small, suffocating room filled with invoices and statements and documents. A few scraps of paper sit in front of me – the remains of my fiction created the previous evening.

There's silence.

I look at his picture again. At my smiley, oversized blue head, and my long clawed arms. It's an odd thing, about children's drawings. At some stage in their lives, almost every child will draw a picture of themselves, surrounded by their families. And the results are paradoxical. They're the ugliest, most treasured things in the world. The figures I'm looking at are deformed, hideous. They glare at me with mismatched eyes and twisted grins. Their limbs are bent in angles that wouldn't be possible for real arms to imitate.

But people never see these horrible things. They only see the child drawing them, and they see the concentration on his little face. They can feel the excitement that he felt when he unveiled it to the two most important people in his life. And they know what it represents. A feeling of belonging, of security.

I feel happiness and sadness in equal measure. Happiness remembering that time, sadness that it's over. That it will never be like it was.

*

I talked to him for a good hour today. It was his birthday. He's eleven now. I didn't mean it to, but talk turned to the divorce. It had just been on my mind, with him being away. I asked him whether he remembered what it had been like when Mum and I had been together. And of course he said no.

Thinking this, fresh tears well up in my eyes. Six of the most important years in my whole life, and he barely remembers them. I want to pick him up and shake him. I want to hold him. I want those years to mean something to him.

I want him here with me.

But none of those things can happen.

I lash out suddenly, sending a pile of paper fluttering into the air. I pick up a stapler, hurling it at the door. It hits it with a bang.

I pick up my pen, and turn my attention to the paper on my desk.

And that's when it happens.

My skin changes colour. I watch with horror as the flesh darkens, turning a full-bodied black within seconds. I know what this means. But not now, it can't happen now. Not at this time. There are too many people!

My chest tightens, and my breathing becomes ragged. I look at the window, at the reflection of myself. I watch as my eyes turn black, and then widen until they are the size of golf balls. I open my mouth. Jagged teeth line my gums, and my tongue has become thinner, longer. My nose disappears as my face elongates. My eyes are pushed to either side of my head, like a bird's.

Or a reptile's.

I fall off my chair, my yells turning hoarse and guttural. It's taking over. My fingers rake at the desk, my sharp digits elongating into claws. A tail bursts from my back, tearing my shirt. I feel every bone creak as it stretches to breaking point, and then thickens. I yell again, but what emerges from my mouth is a roaring shriek. My shirt falls from my scaly chest, and that's when I lose control. The Creature is back.

And it wants Alex.

I watch from a corner of my own mind as it struggles to its feet. Remains of my clothes dangle from its body, but it makes no attempt to dislodge them. Even from the recesses of my own head, I still manage to retain control over some amount of my own dignity.

It shrieks again, a sound that echoes throughout the entire house. Something bangs on the floor. I know who it is. It's Mr Dudley, with his trusty broom in hand. The Creature thinks about killing him, but I manage to direct its attention away. We want Alex.

It doesn't bother opening the door, instead charging straight for it. The door offers very little resistance. The next second, one of its bulbous eyes is fixed on the couple across the hall, the students who have just moved in. They had been kissing passionately when we made our exit. The Creature considers killing them too. It is angry on my behalf. But this time it needs no coaxing from me. It faces the banister, and jumps.

Three storeys are no problem. It hits the tiling with a crack. It's the tiling that's broken. Nothing can hurt the Creature. It's invincible. And it knows where it's going. It knows what it wants.

As it hurtles towards the doors, I can still feel the power of a body that's no longer mine. A long reptilian body. Black, scaly, impenetrable skin. Powerful legs propelling us towards the door, with two long, clawed toes. Two muscular arms that the Creature never quite got used to. It attempts to tuck them under its body when it runs, but that feel somehow slightly off. It's my control that does that, the embodiment of those dinosaur documentaries I watched as a child. Long, snapping jaws, and a rectangular head. Small, horizontally pointed ears. Two large black eyes, one on either side of its head. They're the only thing about it that seems more insect-like than reptilian. Like a housefly. All-seeing.

It hammers through the second door, out onto the street.

People panic. Cars career into lampposts, into buildings, into each other. Pedestrians scream, forming tightly packed hordes that thunder in the other direction.

People start dying.

Some get trampled by the crowds. Some get mown down by cars. The Creature notices one man stray onto the nearby train tracks. It sees him climb the fence, and then not quite manage to hop the rails. The electricity courses through his body, and he falls. He lies there, twitching, until the Creature looks away. It doesn't care. Neither do I. We only want Alex.

Alex is several miles away, but that doesn't matter. We know where to go. The Creature has witnessed me drive this distance countless times, and even after five years, I still secretly think of it as home.

We collapse again, shrieking. I know what the Creature is doing. It's necessary, but it still hurts. I can feel the bones forming behind my back, the muscles interweaving between them. They feel tight, constricted.

And then the Creature unfurls its wings, and I experience an intense relief. I always hate that part. I'm always afraid something will go wrong, that the muscles will mesh into the Creature's flesh, or something hideous will happen –

The Creature cuts me off. It has no voice, but I know the question that it's asking me.

What now?

And I tell it.

*

I see Diane. We're outside the window. The Creature got us here with very little difficulty. It can be quiet when it wants to be. She's with a man. A new one. She hasn't known him longer than a few weeks. Danny. I've only met him once. He didn't say much. Nervous kid. About twenty years my junior. He's only fifteen years older than Alex, for the love of Christ. Twenty-five. That alone is enough for me not to like him.

The Creature growls quietly when it recognises him. I soothe it. Not yet. I want to listen first. We're right next to the window, but the Creature's skin melds well with the dark of the night, and they can't see us. We can see them, though, cuddled up on the sofa. The TV is off. They're talking.

"I just worry about him, is all." murmured Diane.

"Why?" Danny asked. "He's a grown man. He can take care of himself."

"We should have...I don't know, we should have had counselling or something."

"For what? You were splitting up."

"Don't be so ignorant, Dan." she scowled. "I know he doesn't make the best first impression, but he's still Alex's father. I can't just dismiss him from my life."

"Baby, I wasn't suggesting that." Danny soothes her. I retch inwardly. Baby? She's a thirty-eight year old woman, for Christ's sake.

"All I'm saying," Danny continued, "is that you have to move on. It's not healthy for Alex. He can sense stuff like that."

Listen to him. I muttered to the Creature. Talking like he knows Alex.

The Creature doesn't reply. It can't. But I know it agrees.

"The past is the past, and Alex's dad is quite capable of getting help for himself if he wants it."

"He won't." Diane shook her head. "I know him. He won't admit he needs it."

"Then why are you worrying yourself to start with?"

"Because he does need help! And because I care, Danny!" She was annoyed now. "Just because you don't know him, you think he doesn't matter. If you're serious about this relationship, you have to contend with him, because I'm not shutting him out of Alex's life. Neither of them deserve that."

"I don't have any problem with him." said Danny. He said it calmly. I could almost believe him. "I just think you shouldn't fixate so much. He has his own life."

"He doesn't see Alex enough."

"Then he needs to make more of an effort." said Danny firmly. "From what I know of him, he just sits in his study, moping."

She nodded grimly.

"Cheer up." he smiles. He pecks her on the cheek.

They look at each other.

They start to kiss.

The Creature tears through that window like it's paper, sending glass fragments spiralling across the room. Danny and Diane leap away from each other. They are frozen for a second.

The Creature shrieks, a roaring howl that shakes the foundations of the house.

Danny grabs a poker from the fireplace. It is cold, but it's the closest thing to hand.

"Run!" he yells. His voice is so childish.

We run at him. He pushes Diane away, but doesn't even have time to swing the poker before we're on him. The Creature claws at his face. He screams. Chunks of flesh come away in our palms. It's almost too easy.

It doesn't take long for Danny to stop screaming. Twenty seconds, if that. After a minute, there isn't a lot left to identify him as human.

The Creature turns its head towards Diane. The blood is dripping from its chin. I hate that. I try to raise a hand to wipe it away, but the Creature stops me. It needs me to concentrate on something else.

Diane is still silent. She is still staring at Danny's remains.

The words are difficult to form in the Creature's mouth. I have trouble wrapping our reptilian tongue around them. But somehow I manage. Four simple words.

"Where is my son?"

After a second or two, she points. He is standing at the door. He watches us.

"What – ?"

It's him. We've found him. We've been looking for him, and now we've found him.

The Creature runs at Alex, barrelling Diane aside. I don't want to hurt her, but as long as she's not harmed, I don't care. I only have eyes for my son.

We scoop him up in our powerful arms. We turn towards the shattered window, unfurling our wings as we go. Alex is still silent.

Diane screams as we leap, and take flight. We're taking him away. To where he should be – with his father.

We fly. I hear him laugh – he is enjoying himself. We roll and loop in the air, his giggles echoing in our ears. The Creature purrs.

We fly.

And we fly.

And we fly.

*

I put the pen down. The stories get longer and more fantastical each time I write them. But they never bring Alex back to me. He still lives with Diane, and Danny. And he still doesn't remember those six years.

There's nothing I can do about it.

They're living their happy lives, and I'm sat here in a dark room, living in a fantasy world.

I hurl my pen across the room. It bounces off the window with an unsatisfying click. I looked around the room, my eyes finally coming to rest on a photoframe of Diane and me. I don't know why I still have it. We're divorced. I pick it up and launch it at the wall. It smashes, the glass cracking and falling in fragments to the floor.

But the destruction doesn't make me feel any better. I know what I have to do. I have to talk to Alex.

It was probably past his bedtime. But I need to talk to him. I need to.

I pick up the phone.

And I start to cry.

A Well-used Path

Clive

The path was rather exposed. To our right, vertical rocks towered over us; to our left, a vertical drop of several hundred feet to the sea. I'm not very good with heights at the best of times. But the ground was firm, and the path was wide and level, and the weather was fine.

The cliff curved gently leftward, so we could see a mile or more of the path, following the same ledge all the way around the curve until it disappeared around the headland. We knew it was a well-used path.

As we got further around the curve, the ledge got progressively narrower. Here and there there were short stretches where, rather than a level surface of solid rock, there was a grass surface sloping steeply towards the sea, with a narrow muddy track incised into the grass. But by then, we weren't all that far from the headland, and we could see the path quite clearly all the way – there were a few more such stretches, but they didn't look any worse than this one. We could see the notch in the skyline where the path went around the headland; the path was wide there and on solid rock. And we knew it was a well-used path.

It really didn't get any worse all the way to the headland.

Then we reached the headland. The view from that wide rocky platform at the point was superb in the sunshine, back to the village along the path we'd just walked, and across the sea to the next island, where clouds were playing around the tops of the mountain.

The path continued wide and level around the headland. After a hundred metres or so we could see into the next bay – another cliff face curving gently leftward, very like the first. Except that here there wasn't a single ledge all the way around to the next headland. There were several parallel ledges, five or ten metres apart vertically, and none of them extended all the way from this headland to the next. The ledge we were on gave out around three hundred metres around the cliff, and we could see how the path was a steep scramble down to the next ledge, fifty metres or so before the end of our ledge.

When we arrived at the vertical scramble, we could see that it was a man-made stone staircase, partly chiselled out of the rock face, and partly built up onto the lower ledge with large stone blocks. Grass was growing in the cracks in the stone, and the surface of the stone was smoothed and indented from the wear of hundreds of years of foot traffic. It was clearly safe enough, but very exposed. It was hard to overcome my fear. I was very careful descending that short staircase.

This second ledge was longer, but wide and safe feeling, and took us within fifty metres of the next headland. At that point, there was a very similar staircase twenty metres upwards to another ledge. Going up wasn't so difficult, even though the stairs were longer. The next ledge was mostly a transverse grass slope with a narrow muddy track, but it wasn't very far to the second headland, and another wide platform.

From the headland we could see another curve of cliff to yet a third headland. Far beyond the third headland we could see the coast curving leftward again, but much lower, a wide grassy area with a low cliff down to the sea, and a surfaced road well back from the cliff edge. We realized the next village must be just around the next corner of the cliff.

But this curve of cliff looked far more menacing than the first two. The ledge was much narrower, and there were more places where we had to climb up or down from one ledge to another. Halfway around the curve, a narrow cleft cut into the rock, and the ledge disappeared into it. There was no corresponding ledge coming out the other side. We couldn't tell from the headland whether the path continued on a lower or a higher ledge. But we knew it was a well-used path.

Before we got to the cleft, the sun disappeared behind a cloud. Then the top of the cliffs on our right disappeared in a shroud of mist. But the path was still clear, and we were well below the cloud line.

It wasn't very light inside the cleft, and the rocks were damp and a bit slick. The cleft curved slightly to the right, so we couldn't see how far into the cliff it went, and we still couldn't see whether we went up or down to the next ledge. The ledge below us on the far side of the cleft didn't look to have a path along it, really, so we assumed we must go up somehow.

We rounded the curve. The path went down another staircase ahead of us. Further on, the cleft continued, but there was a wide rock bridge joining the sides of the cleft, with a ledge on each side of the cleft going both ways, deeper into the cleft and back out to the open sea. We could hear the waves crashing between the rock walls far below us.

The ledge on the far side of the cleft, back towards the sea, didn't appear to have a path along it. The path seemed to go back along the ledge below the one we'd arrived on, but that made no sense. We set off along the ledge that obviously went the way we wanted to go. It was wet and narrow and there was moss growing on it, and it really didn't feel safe at all. But it was the obvious way forward. In places we had to go on our hands and knees.

It became impossible. It was simply too narrow. We had to turn back. Turning wasn't easy, we had to reverse a few metres before we could. At the rock bridge we pondered our next move. Should we admit defeat, and head back to the village?

We decided to try the way the path seemed to lead on, however illogical a route it seemed. It was a much less dangerous ledge than the one we'd just been defeated by, and we could always get back easily enough.

We'd almost reached the end of the cleft before we saw the solution to the conundrum. The path went down another set of stairs, and then someone had built an arch across the cleft to a ledge on the other side. It was a very solid bridge constructed of large stone blocks without mortar – but quite narrow, especially at the summit, and with no parapet. We went over on our hands and knees. Descending the far side was terrifying.

Round the final headland, the path descended in a series of staircases and ledges, zigzagging back and forth across the face of the cliff. This cliff didn't descend all the way to the sea, but to a grassy cirque with the village nestling at its centre. The road we'd seen ended at the village.

The sea cliffs had been pretty solid rock, but this cliff was crumbling in places. Some sections of the path had evidently fallen away, and been repaired. The repairs didn't look nearly as sound as the ancient, original construction. Here and there pieces of rock moved slightly underfoot.

Then there was a section where the path hadn't been repaired at all following what looked like a recent rockfall. We could see the path continuing five metres away, diagonally below us, but the only way to reach it was to scramble down the loose boulders of the rockfall, and back up the other side. It felt very precarious, but we managed.

It looked straightforward from that point – we could see the path ahead all the way down to the grass, and it all looked undamaged.

I'd been bringing up the rear all the way. As Mike, just in front of me, stepped onto a rock halfway down a set of stairs, it shifted under his foot. He grabbed at a handhold in the rock wall to his right, and a large stone came out in his hand. He jumped for the next step as the boulder under him tumbled away, and managed to grab hold of another bit of the rock face. Which held. He was safe.

But the tumbling boulder hit another rock below, and dislodged that. The second rock fell, and undermined a whole section of the cliff. I felt the staircase trembling beneath me, and scrambled back up to the top and onto the ledge we'd just come along just in time. My friends ran down the stairs onto the next ledge. The whole staircase collapsed, leaving a sheer drop between where I was and where my friends were. There was no way we could possibly cross.

There was no choice. They had to go on to the next village, and I had to go back. Three miles along all those ledges, and alone across that narrow bridge.

It was beginning to rain, and the cloud line was descending above me.

The Stair

John

As I was walking up the stair

It's frustrating. I've been living in this house for some time now; it and I have a lot of history together. I grew up here, played in the garden with my younger sister Emma; watched TV in the lounge, enthralled as Jerry outsmarted Tom for the umpteenth time before the early evening news came on. This is my home – I can't imagine being anywhere else. The thing is that it's comfortable; not too big, at least it never seems so, but not so small as to feel cramped inside. I'd stay here forever if I could; it is home – that simple.

The house itself is detached, built in the 1920s in a quiet residential area of the town, at the top of a hill and near a railway cutting. Opposite was the main gate of the towns Girls School, something that meant nothing to me when we first moved in and I was ten. But some few years later the slightly older lad I had become had cause to be thankful for my front facing bedroom window. Perhaps it's best to leave it at that, except to say that I was grateful for my parents having net curtains on every window. It's a nice house in a nice area, and as far as I know, nothing "nasty" has ever happened there.

I met a man who wasn't there.

However this particular night, something just didn't feel right. I was going upstairs that evening preparing for bed, and it was as if someone invisible had brushed passed me. The stairs creaked before I got to them, and it was as if a light breeze was blowing into my face. I shivered momentarily and suddenly felt like I was being watched. I'd never felt like that before.

No, I tell a lie; I have.

I was about eleven years old, and in my old bedroom. It was a small room, but comfortable. I had my shelves around the wall above the bed, filled with my favourite books (indomitable Gauls with their magic potion thwarting the roman geezer... Ha!) and a half completed model railway on my table. Life was good, and I had no reason to even consider the possibility that it could ever be otherwise.

I remember waking up at the dead of night with shivers starting to wrack my body. There was someone there, I was certain of it. At the foot of my bed, there was somebody there. I felt freezing cold, regardless of the warm covers around me, and the shivers just wouldn't stop. I was scared; so very, very, scared. I couldn't move - I dare not, in case such action would cause the unseen presence to rouse from its stillness and move towards me.

And so I stayed for what seemed ages; honestly I don't know how long it lasted – shaking, terrified, not daring to move. Suddenly the horrific sensations stopped just as abruptly as they had started, and the room seemed instantly to return to normal. I recall simply turning over and going back to sleep, just as easily as that.

There – that is my ghost story. Every kid has one in one form or another – and it is the only ghost story I've really had. Until now, that is.

He wasn't there again today

It was this – a sudden memory of an old childhood incident – that truly gave me pause on the staircase. Not so much a return to the terror felt so fiercely all those years ago, but perhaps more a remembrance of an innocent age. Instead of going straight to my current bedroom (over the garage, overlooking the garden), I decided to visit my old room.

Of course it's all changed now; an office where I sometimes sit in an uncomfortable chair in front of an outdated computer, and struggle with spreadsheets, databases and occasionally bandwidth as I try to get that last Orc slain. Not tonight though.

The moon is shining through the window, overlooking the houses that replaced the school decades ago. I stand there, at the window, staring at the spot where the bed used to be; remembering all that has happened in the time since that evening. Perhaps it's the memory of how scared I felt that night, but my thoughts run dark and deep. All the bad things come to mind; things that would be less than 5 years ahead in my younger self's future. The worst time of my life, the darkest time.

What would I say to my younger self, if he was there, right now? I talk into the moonlight; I address the kid that would become me. I talk about Yorkshire and the school and plead with them not to trust a certain older boy one summer Sunday afternoon. I talk about hurt silence, betrayal and a different sort of fear. Of self-loathing and the importance of speaking out.

I plead with him, cajole him; imagining him there in bed, trying desperately to make them understand through the barrier of so many years. I'm shaking, feeling cold, regardless of the warmth of the room around me; and the shivers just don't stop. I'm scared; so very, very, scared of saying aloud what has festered in my heart for so long. I can't stop - I dare not. Now that I've started it has to be said, no matter how much it hurts. "Please," I say: "Please, don't become me! Please be someone better, someone stronger…" The tears are rolling down my cheeks, and dry racking sobs replace all words. I can't stay in the room any longer.

I stumble back down the stairs, go to the kitchen and make myself a cup of tea. I sit at the breakfast bar, still crying and shaking. It can't be all so bad, can it? Has my life been so defined by what happened to me all those years ago?

Yes – yes it has been. If I could go back and change things, I would. Even if it meant the entire life I've lived from that point onward no longer existing, I would still do it.

So there I sit – the ghost of a man crippled by events, circumstances, and an inability to forget and move on. A man that shouldn't exist, and if there was any justice in the world, wouldn't need to.

I wish that man would go away.

Bunker VI

Stephen

And so we reach a climax. Who will get the chair? Will Howard get to fire his gun? Is there in fact any humus in the Bunker? Well, actually this shouldn't be quite as tense and unexpected as you might think. Colin has a secret.

When he first found the Bunker he was content to simply wander around eating the free food. But as he came to know the place better he had other ideas. These ideas mostly revolved around the hydroponics units. But in order to make full use of them he needed to be able to change the day/night cycle. You see a marijuana plant can grow in a normal cycle, but to get maximum yield and strength in a shorter time it is better to force upon them a more rapid cycle. Colin was aware of this and felt that if he were going to do it then he may as well do it properly.

But changing the day/night cycle would require someone in a position of authority. At first he considered making himself the Head Gardener. After all, that was all the authority he'd need. But as he learned more about what he was about to do and the benefits of it he realised that he may as well be hung for a sheep as a lamb and opted to make himself the RECC Senior Officer. He did not find the command key that Desmond now possesses. That is a highly illegal spare. No, he took a more direct route and inadvertently helped himself out at the same time.

The proper procedure upon entering the Bunker involves the new residents taking receipt of their Bunker Key as they enter. The walls of the main entry way are covered in recessed shelving. Our residents would have noticed that had Colin not destroyed the opening mechanism in an effort to force them open. Had they opened smoothly as the main doors opened then perhaps it could have been noticed that a few of them were missing.

It should be pointed out that there are only two hundred keys. The Bunker has capacity for over two thousand occupants.

The four occupants arrive in the Command Centre at the same time. Both Mary and Colin are quick to notice the increased level of firepower in the room. But of the two only Colin could tell you exactly what it was and how accurate it would be in Call of Duty. Desmond does as he is used to doing and takes charge of the situation.

DESMOND – Right, what have you been able to find out?

MARY – What's with the gun?

DESMOND – Ignore that for the moment, lets concentrate on getting out of here shall we?

COLIN – So we don't need the gun, he can put it down.

Colin has returned to using the chair as a shield.

DESMOND – I've already been through all this with Howard. He *is* the senior security officer

Mary is so amazed by this statement that she is unable to form a coherent response.

DESMOND – Now.

With a flourish he brings his Command key out and cocks his head in what he believes is a jaunty manner. He is wrong.

DESMOND – We need to make use of this, did you find anything out?

MARY – Well, yes. Upon opening the bunker each upper tier resident is assigned a key. That key is then fingerprint locked to its owner.

DESMOND – Fingerprint locked?

MARY – Yeah, press the button on the top, state your name and service number and the key locks to you.

HOWARD – Really? What if you pick up the wrong key?

MARY – Well there are ways to change it, mostly within the first twenty four hours of activation but after that only a senior key can override it.

DESMOND – Ok, so…

MARY – Hey wait a second.

He presses the button on top, nothing happens.

DESMOND – Perhaps the system needs to be online?

MARY – Look are we sure that you are the one who should use that thing?

DESMOND – Of course, I have seniority here.

MARY – Well yes but you've hardly got the technological skill required to…

DESMOND – I am the only one who has received training for this kind of situation, and I *am* the senior authority figure here.

With surprising grace Desmond ignores the snort of derision from Colin.

MARY – I hardly think a weekend's training course in Gretna covers This!

HOWARD – Oh what does it matter, we just need to get out of here. And you said yourself we have twenty four hours to change it if we have to.

MARY – Well yes but….

DESMOND – We need to find out what's going on, and this is how we do it.

He gestures to the Playstation. As we watch this scene unfold take note of Colin who is looking extra shifty. He has not taken his eyes of Howard who in turn has been slowly manoeuvring himself closer to Colin.

A few moments pass as Mary reluctantly disconnects the alien hardware from the system and it in turn reboots. As before the red emergency lighting activates.

BUNKER – All occupants to designated work stations. Security Protocols are in effect.

DESMOND – Aha!

BUNKER – All occupants to designated work stations. Stand By for orders from RECC Senior Officer. Security Protocols are in effect.

Desmond steps toward the command chair and is confused as once again, nothing happens.

Shaking it for a moment, in the manner of one who believes this will somehow work, he then presses the button again. Still nothing.

BUNKER – Warning, Warning. RECC Senior Officer to command centre.

DESMOND – I'm *in* the bloody command centre!

With a tinge of desperation he begins to examine the device more closely while muttering something about 'batteries.'

BUNKER – Warning, Warning. RECC Senior Officer to command centre immediately.

A high pitch squeal fills the room and then is suddenly stopped.

BUNKER – Good evening Commander Shepard, RECC6 awaits your orders.

Three of the residents look around in confusion. One just looks a bit sheepish.

On the main screen a large face appears behind which is a fully functioning and staffed control room. It is slightly, well no, in all honesty, *a lot* more up to date than ours.

RECC1 CONTROL – Ahh RECC6, we were beginning to think we had lost you!

HOWARD – Who the hell are you?

RECC1 CONTROL – I'm Paul, the communications officer for RECC1.

Paul's cheesy grin is not helped by the vastness of the main screen.

RECC1 CONTROL – Oh dear, you haven't the faintest idea what's going on do you?

Straightening his jacket and wiping a hand across his head Desmond steps forward.

DESMOND – Ah, Desmond Hayne, Senior Officer, if I may?

RECC1 CONTROL – Hayne? Where's Shepard?

DESMOND – Shepard?

RECC1 CONTROL – Commander Shepard is registered as the commanding officer at RECC6.

From behind the control chair Colin raises a hand.

COLIN – Erm, that would be me

DESMOND, HOWARD, MARY – What?!

RECC1 CONTROL – Ah excellent, and how many people were you able to save?

Note the way Paul utterly disregards the shabbiness of Colin.

COLIN – Erm… four?

RECC1 CONTROL – Four?? How unfortunate… Would you excuse me while I inform my superiors?

MARY – No wait! What happened?

RECC1 CONTROL – You don't know? Of course you don't know. Well, actually we aren't sure either. But one thing is certain, life as we know it has ended. You're lucky to have survived. The Earth has suffered a Near Extinction Event.

MARY – Near?

RECC1 CONTROL – Well, we're alive aren't we?

The enormous face of Paul vanishes and is replaced by the system status screen. This has all sorts of useful information on it including the dubious status of the Bunker's power supply. But sadly no one is paying it the slightest attention. Desmond is standing stunned, too shaken even to whimper. Mary is clinging to the back of Howard who in turn has finally managed to get hold of Colin and is gleefully trying to wring his neck.

For Whom the Bluebells

Tracey

Bob and Steve were enjoying their Sunday morning tour through an area with which they were thoroughly familiar. Some of the route involved trekking through an ancient, picturesque bridleway.

About midway into this route, (essentially a tree-tunnel traversing up a large hill), they stopped briefly to take photos.

They'd both been this way many times. It looked different each time, depending on the time of day and season.

They had a drink of water and surveyed newly germinated wheat visible between the April foliage which encompassed them.

Opposite the wheat fields, a mist of bluebells rose like purple smoke, from deep within the woodland side of the bridleway.

And it was here the pair split up. They agreed to meet in one hour at a local village pub. Bob stayed on to take photos of the bluebell wood as Steve vanished quickly over the top of the hill and out of sight.

An hour passed, and the cyclist who had left his companion behind, relaxed and waited for his photographer-friend to catch up and enjoy a pint.

Another half-hour passed. Steve sent a text to Bob, but his friend's phone was off. After waiting a reasonable time, Steve decided perhaps something happened and back-tracked along the route.

Steve arrived to the spot he felt certain they had both stopped.

There was no sign of his friend.

It was afternoon now and the light had changed. Steve tried a text message again, but was out of range. He was fairly certain this was the place. Those tyre tracks and footprints were theirs alright.

So where was Bob?

He shouted Bob's name. A sudden breeze blew. Dappled light from between the branches moved along the ground. It seemed like something was moving deep inside the wood. He could almost swear there was something. Were his eyes playing tricks on him?

Shouting again, then listening. Steve thought he heard something. His ears strained to hear. He cursed. He cursed again, feeling Bob was obviously being an inconsiderate lout for not at least sending a text message to say what was going on.

So, with that heated thought, Steve pedalled off hard down the track.

Five minutes further along, Steve encountered a mixed-group of about seven walkers. He guessed they were mostly in their fifties. They were all clothed appropriately with good shoes, sticks & hats. With them, were two dogs: a poodle and a Labrador.

Steve asked the walkers if they had seen his mate, Bob. They listened and shook their heads. No cyclists since before noon. And none matching Bob's description.

Steve carried on cycling down the hill. He was in a hurry to get back home.

Not so very long after Steve left, a black horse and blank-faced male rider approached the walkers on the track.

They all moved politely aside as you are supposed to, but in this case it was more so as not to get trampled. He was not dressed in riding clothes, but wore a narrow leather case on his back held by a leather strap running diagonally across his chest.

Oddly, the rider made no acknowledgement nor gave thanks. He didn't wave hello, even, which is standard politeness on meeting strangers on any trail. Why imagine! He failed to greet the group! When this rider was well out of earshot, each one of the walkers noted the weirdness. Quite unnerving.

Steve got home, checked his phone for messages. Nothing. Bob's girlfriend, Lisa, sent a text asking Steve to tell Bob to call.

24 hours later Bob officially became a missing person and the police spent a long time talking to Steve about it. The entire area was searched. The bluebell woods were trampled, as was the young wheat field. Police appealed to the walkers, who came forward.

In 1790, a man named Robert Breddell was set upon, allegedly, for poaching deer. He was hung along the bridleway, then buried in secret, under an ancient bluebell wood.

Through the years, there have been many sightings of his ghost, and the occasional report of a mounted archer still shooting deer in the wood from atop a black horse.

Attrition

Jack

Ladies and gentlemen, assorted species, thank you. I'm humbled to receive such a warm welcome on an alien homeworld, so far from my native land. A special thanks to my fellow humans among you, and the Martian Council for their hospitality, which makes tonight possible.

As I stand before you today, I do not see Humans. I do not see Martians. I see no divisions, no enforced arbitrary lines that would cut our societies down the middle. I find myself in this bastion of Martian culture, a magnificent symbol of union between our two races. A construct of human and alien origin, pooling collective knowledge to build a dream our forefathers would barely have thought imaginable.

Yet above and around us, a war rages between Men and Martians. A war of ignorance, intolerance and injustice. Countless billions on both worlds are kept to ransom for the actions of the fraction in power. I see parents lose their children, and children lose their parents. Brothers, sisters, uncles and aunts, grand-parents and cousins. None are safe as the Vacuum Wars descend upon my planet, consuming all like a living thing, a manifestation of the greed that befalls sentience.

Those who do not die are radicalized. Grief begets blame, blame begets violence. The eyes of planet Earth turn to Mars with a vengeful hatred, and the recruiting stations overflow with the widowed and orphaned. On the other side of the mirror, Martians flood in droves to their armouries and their hangars in a final, desperate attempt to end the threat of the Human menace.

Tonight, here in this room, we are something different. We are the people who recognise right from wrong. We are the people who will stand up and cry no, and fly in the face of a ubiquitous fury that suffocates both our races. We realise the scope of the opportunity that faces us – through some slip of fate, some freak accident of chance, we find ourselves occupying two planets in the same small corner of this infinite universe, against the vast and arbitrary rules of time, space and evolution. Our species would waste it, and spit in the face of the infinite, benevolent mechanisms of the universe, in spite of the wonderful gift it has given us: the knowledge that we are not alone.

We may be persecuted, and we may be hushed, but we will not be silenced. We have an idea, my friends, and as the idiom goes – ideas cannot be killed. We must throw off the primitive shackles of hate and bigotry, and embrace the mantles granted to civilized societies. We stand stronger together than we do divided, engaged in senseless conflicts based on twisted prejudices. The proof towers above us – a building beyond the realms of the deepest dreams of those that came before us, resisting forces that they could not even conceive.

Together, we know what we can accomplish – with peace, friendship and an extended hand, we can conquer the overpowering forces of Nature itself. Our ancestors looked to the stars and wondered what the future held. And I come tonight to tell you that it is us.

We are the future. War is destitute, and it is obsolete. We are the vanguard that will bring peace to this tiny corner of our universe, and usher forward a new era, in which Martians and mankind are a single entity, marked by our bond for one another.

And on that day, my brothers, our voices will be heard across the stars.

On that day, my brothers, unity will reign.

On that day, my brothers, WE WILL BE CAPABLE OF ANYTHING.

My Head is like a Circus

Lovie Lovetree

Where does this shit come from?
The lion tamer saying that he's going to quit
the clown weeps in the corner
and the girls are in the air
swinging higher than they should
what a dangerous game
the elephants are raging
the doves have flown away
the bunnies eat the meat of the manager
and the tent is torn
the colour shifting lights
hanging far too low
horses in a trapeze
drunk belly dancers
unicycling in the audience seats
at least there's no audience
there's no time for embarrassment like this
popping balloons
confetti everywhere
get your shit together you idiots
train the snails
teach me how to dance
or just put me in the cannon
and fire me out of here

The Authors

Some of us are family; we're all friends. Some of us were at school together in the 1960s, or were housemates in the 1970s.

Some of us only know each other online, through *deviantart.com*, an art community, or through *justthetalk.com*, a forum that was originally a sort of lifeboat for survivors of the sinking of the good ship *Guardian User Talk*, a forum created by the Guardian newspaper for its readers and then, after a few years, summarily destroyed by them for Reasons Apparently Best Left Obscure.

Our ages range from the early twenties to the early eighties.

Most of us are native English speakers, but Grace's mother-tongue is Hindi, Lovie's is Icelandic, Marko's is Croatian, and Meryem's is French. We all wrote in English apart from Meryem, whose story Clive translated with her approval.

There's a bit of background to Rosie's story. It's actually her great-grandmother's words. Rosie submitted it to the school magazine in about 1965, but it was rejected. The eldest son in the story was Rosie's grandfather, killed in the first world war shortly before Rosie's mother was born.

Harry's is also a true story – obviously with names changed!

And if you can make sense of the cover in relation to the stories, do let us know. Some of it's probably obvious – but…

www.ingramcontent.com/pod-product-compliance
Lightning Source LLC
Chambersburg PA
CBHW060936180626
46817CB00004B/1569